I0593999

Finding True Home

Sequel to Seeking the American Dream

Heidi M. Thomas

SunCatcher Publications

Praise for *Finding True Home*

"Following the Moser family through life in Montana is a delightful journey. But life is full of pain and sorrow as well as love and laughter. Struggling to find her place in America, Anna has more than her share of each. –Sally Harper Bates, award-winning author of *Life Between Dust & Clouds* and *Ponderings*

"This sequel to *Seeking the American Dream* continues Heidi Thomas' heart-tugging saga of the life of a World War II war bride as she struggles to adjust to life on a Montana ranch, where family is everything and neighbor helps neighbor through the toughest situations. Struggling through isolation, prejudice, and self-doubt, Anna Moser finally finds peace, acceptance, and her true home through a lifetime of love and sacrifice." – Donis Casey, author of the Alafair Tucker series

"*Finding True Home* is the author's fictional story of her mother, a woman who immigrated from Germany after World War II. Transplanted to a difficult life on a Montana ranch, she finds everything foreign, and believes the neighbors there do not trust her. While she is different, she holds on to feeling that way long after people have ceased to notice. She raises three children who all differ in personality and tries to hold them close, long after they have flown the nest. Thomas makes the events of life seem very personal. Watching the older generation dying off and the new one taking their place, moved this reviewer to tears many times. This coming of age story of an adult woman makes you realize it is never too late for love to triumph." –Linda Jacobs, author of the "Yellowstone" series novels

"This addition to Heidi M Thomas's body of work is sure to captivate readers as much as previous books in the series. She gives readers rich and accurate accounts of obstacles young women faced eighty - ninety years ago. Young women who desperately wanted to step out of society's restrictive molds. Thomas shows us how Montana women aspiring to participate in male dominated roles faced their fears and naysayers with determination and courage." – Karen Casey-Fitzjerrell, author of *Forgiving Effie Beck* and *The Dividing Season*

Other books by Heidi M. Thomas

Cowgirl Dreams series
Cowgirl Dreams
Follow the Dream
Dare to Dream

American Dream series
Seeking the American Dream
Finding True Home

Nonfiction
Cowgirl Up! A History of Rodeo Women

Praise for *Seeking the American Dream*

"Heidi Thomas's latest novel grips the reader from the first opening sentence, as her nurse-protagonist struggles to face the wretched suffering in war-torn Hamburg during the final days of WWII. From there, her sweeping saga takes her away from Europe's lurching efforts to rebuild, and into the building of her own new life in America. From the perspective of a hard-working, and still bright-eyed young woman, we participate in America's own next chapter." –Mara Purl, best-selling author of the Milford-Haven Novels

"Once again, I open the pages of a Heidi Thomas novel and I'm transported to another time and place. From post WWII Germany to the sometimes-brutal Montana ranch life, Seeking the American Dream explores one woman's journey as she faces impossible odds to live her dream. Ms. Thomas is excellent at period literature. You won't be disappointed."—Brenda Whiteside, Author of The Love and Murder Series

Seeking the American Dream is such a beautiful, heartwarming book! It was a pleasure to read about Anna's quest for her dream. I didn't just enjoy it, I loved it! Heidi Thomas has a way of building suspense that just kills me. Readers will love it as much as I do. –Carol Buchanan, award-winning author of "The Vigilante Quartet."

Praise for the Cowgirl Dreams series

Cowgirl Dreams: "Nettie Brady defies anyone who challenges her right to become a rodeo rider. She'll gladly take the bone-jarring, gut-twisting ride of a wild steer rather than endure the stark boredom of women's work in the 1920s. Needlepoint isn't her thing– horseback riding, working cattle, and, yes, rodeo riding are what her life is all about. But family is important, too, and their disapproval makes for heart-wrenching decisions. Heidi Thomas does a magnificent job of pulling readers into another time, another place. *Cowgirl Dreams* is an exciting read, full of heart and yearnings." —Mary E. Trimble, author of *Rosemount, McClellan's Bluff,* and Spur Award finalist *Tenderfoot*

"…Brings heart, verve and knowledge to her depiction of the intrepid Nettie. A lively look at the ranch women of an almost forgotten West." —Deirdre McNamer, MFA English Professor, University of Montana, *Red Rover, My Russian,* and *One Sweet Quarrel*

Follow the Dream: "I enjoyed this bittersweet novel with its accurate depiction of the lives of cowgirls in 1930s Montana and its tender portrait of a marriage." Mary Clearman Blew, award-winning author of *Jackalope Dreams, All but the Waltz: A Memoir of Five Generations in the Life of a Montana Family,* and *Balsamroot: A Memoir*

"In her poignant tale of Nettie Moser's diligent pursuit of a dream, Heidi Thomas gives a stunning example of what it means to "Cowgirl Up." *Follow the Dream* is a dynamic story of a woman's strength and determination that is sure to inspire as well as entertain.—Sandi Ault, award-winning author of *Wild Sorrow*, in the *WILD* Mystery Series

Dare to Dream: "Finding our place and following our hearts is the moving theme of *Dare to Dream,* a finely-tuned finish to Heidi Thomas's trilogy inspired by the life of her grandmother, an early rodeo-rider. With crisp dialogue and singular scenes we're not only invited into the middle of a western experience of rough stock, riders and generations of ranch tradition, but we're deftly taken into a family drama. This family story takes place beginning in 1941 but it could be happening to families anywhere - and is. Nettie, Jake and Neil struggle to find their place and discover what we all must: life is filled with sorrow and joy: faith, family and friends see us through and give meaning to it all. Nettie, or as Jake calls her, 'Little Gal' will stay in your heart and make you want to re-read the first books just to keep her close. A very satisfying read."—Jane Kirkpatrick, *a New York Times* Bestselling author and WILLA Literary Award winner of *A Flickering Light*

Cowgirl Up: A History of Rodeo Women: The best kind of history lesson; Informative and entertaining. Thomas does a great job of showing the lifestyles of these women in a very male dominated world, and how through hard work and determination they gained the respect of many people not only in the U.S., but throughout the world. You can't help but be impressed with the toughness of these women, who competed even with broken bones and other injuries. An eye-opening look at the world of rodeo, and the accomplishments of these women. –John J. Rust, author of *Arizona's All-Time Baseball Team* and the "Fallen Eagle" series

A SunCatcher Publications book

Cover Design by Jason McIntyre
www.TheFarthestReaches.com

Library of Congress Cataloguing-in-Publication data is available on file.

ISBN - 978-0-9990663-1-7

Printed in the United States of America

10 9 8 7 6 5 4 3 2 1

DEDICATION

I dedicate this book to mothers, those who dedicate their lives to their children, sacrificing their own creature-comforts, needs, and desires at times to protect and raise them up the way they should go.

ACKNOWLEDGMENTS

I thank God for giving me the writing gene, my family for their continued support and encouragement, the teachers and editors who believed in me, my fellow Women Writing the West members, my former critique groups in Washington who encouraged me when I was just starting out, and my present critique group who has given me such valuable feedback: Sally Bates, Barbara Beck, John J. Rust, and Brenda Whiteside. Thank you to my beta readers, Carol Buchanan, Linda Jacobs, and Brenda Whiteside for helping make my work better.

"...Tribulation produces perseverance; perseverance, character; and character, hope." Romans 5:3

CHAPTER ONE

The September sun highlighted the clear blue sky and warmed Anna Moser's heart as she drove the mile and a half from their ranch to the Horse Creek Store for groceries. She breathed in the fresh clean air and smiled.

She'd been smiling a lot since she and the kids returned home from her first trip back to Germany after coming to America ten years ago when WWII ended. Anna had come for a better life… and for love.

She had missed her Mutti terribly, not having seen her family for so long. Finally, this past summer she'd gone back for a three-month visit. Because life had been so difficult, trying to make a living farming and ranching in eastern Montana, she'd come to think perhaps she'd made a mistake by immigrating, that America wasn't the "land of milk and honey" she'd envisioned. But Germany was no longer her home. Her birthplace had changed, and so had she.

Montana was her home—in spite of its harsh climate, sacrifice, and hardships in being accepted. Neil was her home. She came back, once again, for love.

Humming, she went into the store with her list, eight-year-old Monica and two-year-old Kevin in tow.

Mrs. Mitchell, one of the neighbors, stepped from behind an aisle. "There's the world travelers. You sure were gone a long time. My, you folks must've had a wonderful calf crop last fall to be able to afford a three-month vacation in Europe."

Her words stung like a bullwhip lash. Surely that wasn't what the neighbors thought, that she'd gone off on some expensive luxury vacation, just for the heck of it. All these women had their mothers and sisters, their brothers and fathers within thirty miles.

She forced a smile. "It has been ten years since I saw my family. It was time to go."

"Oh. Well then. Must be nice."

Anna's neck and face burned. She wanted so badly to march up to snooty Mrs. Mitchell and tell her to wake up, that there were other people in the world besides her. She took a long breath and turned away. Finishing her shopping, she left the store, her earlier euphoria deflated like a sad, week-old balloon.

~~~

After Monica's first day back at school, Anna, Neil, and Kevin waited for her outside the little one-room schoolhouse. There hadn't been a school nearby until just before Monica turned six, when the Mitchell family with three school-age kids moved to a ranch nearby. Questioning her own language skills, Anna was thankful she hadn't had to continue to teach Monica at home.

The Mitchell kids came out first and dashed off toward the country store, just down the slight rise, where their mother waited.

Monica came out a few minutes later, a frown on her face. "I can't find my Thermos."

"Where did you eat your lunch?" Anna opened the car door.

"Oh, I remember now. I took my milk outside to drink." Monica walked over to the swing set where her Thermos lay. She bent down to pick it up, then snatched her hand back. "Ick." She burst into tears.

Anna jumped out of the car, Neil following. "What's the matter, honey?"

Monica sucked in her sobs and pointed at her Thermos. A huge blob of spit clung to it. "They hate me. They called me a germy German."

Anna put her arms around her daughter and exchanged a tight-lipped look with Neil.

"The kids in Germany were so nice to me, even when I couldn't speak much German, and now I'm home and these kids're bein' mean to me." Monica's sobs renewed.

Neil picked up the Thermos, spun on one heel, and headed up the steps of the schoolhouse. Filled with fear, Anna hurried behind him. *Oh dear, please don't create a scene.*

"Mrs.… uh, Dallas." He held the Thermos out toward the teacher.

She frowned. "What is this?"

Neil's jaw clenched and his shoulders tightened. Anger overcame Anna's fear and she stepped forward. "Your students are bullying my daughter. This has to stop. Now."

Neil explained what the kids had said and what had happened.

Dallas rolled her false teeth around in her mouth as was her habit, and her eyebrows formed an angry V. "Well, this is unacceptable behavior. I will talk to the Mitchell kids and their parents. Don't worry. There'll be no more of that."

Back in the car, Anna held her daughter on her lap and rocked her until the tears were spent. The old pain deep in her heart reawakened. Would it never stop? Ever since she'd arrived in America, so many years ago now, she'd had to bear remarks like that about being German. *Yes, we were enemies during the war. But the war's been over for twelve years.*

The neighbors had all seemed happy to see Anna when she came home from her trip, even had a Welcome Home party for her. She'd thought the old prejudice might be gone after living here for ten years. But the Mitchell family hung on to it, and kids picked up on the adults' attitude and what they said.

Monica blew her nose. "I asked what *they* were, then, 'cause their gramma and grampa came from somewhere—everybody did. We just learned that in history. And Eddy said '*We're* Pennsylvania Dutch,' real snotty like."

"Just ignore them, honey." Anna caressed Monica's hair. "They don't know what they're saying. Do like Jesus did, and forgive them."

"Besides, Pennsylvania Dutch *is* German." Neil smirked. "I bet they don't even know that."

"They made fun of me for being Lutheran, too," Monica sniffed. "They said non-dom'nation is better."

Anna grimaced. "You know, it's our own business where we go to church and what we believe. And they can go to whatever church they want. Just know, in here," she tapped her chest, "that you believe in the same God they do, and Jesus loves all children. From now on, don't tell them anything about church or Germany or anything. Just be polite, don't try to argue with them."

Neil glanced over at Monica. "You are just as good as everyone else. You're no better than they are and they're no better than you."

Inside, Anna boiled. She wanted to drive directly to the Mitchell ranch and yell at them. They were teaching their children to hate, to be intolerant of anyone different. But with that kind of anger, maybe she was being as hateful as they were. Maybe Mrs. Mitchell simply didn't realize what it was like to be so far away from loved ones. *I need to be an example and help Monica not feel resentment toward the neighbor kids. Maybe this second generation can break the mold.*

She swallowed the bitterness and sat with a stony face until they got home.

"This is enough," she seethed to Neil that night after the kids were in bed. "I can't put up with this anymore. They can say what they want to me, but not to my kids."

He put his big weathered hand over hers. "I know. It makes me want to punch someone too. But... we both know that won't solve things or make it any more peaceful for any of us."

"It's been twelve years since the war ended. How much longer do people have to hate the Germans? I don't want Monica to suffer like I did." Anna sighed and bit back hot tears. "You're right. I know. Doesn't make it easier though."

"No, it doesn't. But going through these tough things and taking the high road will make Monica a better, stronger person."

She closed her eyes. *I sure hope so. Seems like Neil could stand up for his family though.* She didn't see how the problem was solved by doing nothing.

~~~

Their explanations seemed to satisfy Monica, but Anna could tell she no longer enjoyed going to school as much as she once had. She didn't say a lot about what happened during the day or what she learned, but buried herself in her books when she came home.

One afternoon, Monica staggered out to the car after school, barely able to see over the stack of books she carried.

Anna rushed to help her. "Oh, my goodness. Where'd you get all those books? How many do you have?"

"Only thirty, Mommy. The bookmobile was here today and it won't be back for another *whole month*."

"Just like your daddy. I'm proud of you, honey." A whole month's worth of books. Anna had to turn away to keep Monica from seeing the laughter that bubbled up from her chest to her lips.

After that, Anna knew whenever she hadn't seen her daughter for a while, she would find her in her room, reading. "Come on, honey, you need to do your chores," she'd remind her. Or, "You'd better finish getting ready for school now."

"Okay, Mommy, just a minute." But usually another fifteen or twenty minutes would go by without Monica emerging, and Anna would have to prod her again. And, at night, after the lights were out, she discovered her daughter holding a book up to the window where the yard light shone in.

About that time, Monica started coming home from school with severe headaches and feeling sick to her stomach. "I had that when I was a kid and found out it was my eyesight," Neil said. He and Anna took her to get her eyes tested. Sure enough, she needed glasses.

Anna shook her head. "Well, no wonder. You read in the car, you read in the dark..."

~~~

On a frosty February day in 1959, the old 1940 Buick finally gasped its last smoke-filled breath, and Neil could not cajole another mile out of it with either baling wire or new spark plugs.

Anna laughed at her husband's woeful face. "I'm almost happy it's finally passed away." The seats had long ago lost their cushioning, and she never knew if it was going to start when they had to go somewhere.

"Yeah, I suppose you're right." He grinned sheepishly. "She was a good one, though."

The next week, when his parents Jake and Nettie came to visit, they all drove into Billings to look for another car. A brand new one was out of the question, so they cruised the used car lots, searching for just the right one.

Anna saw it first. "Look, Neil." She pointed to where it shone in the center of the lot as though a spotlight had been placed on it, its two-tone green body glistening. When Neil started the 1956 Ford Galaxy, he turned to Anna with a grin. "She purrs like a kitten." They went for a test drive, made the deal, signed the papers and drove it home. It was as if they had reached the pinnacle of luxury.

The next morning, Anna arose early, as usual, to fix breakfast and get Monica ready for school. She felt more tired than usual, but put it down to their trip to Billings and the excitement of their new car. She had no sooner reached the kitchen when she doubled over and retched into the sink. She wiped her mouth. *Himmel.* Thank goodness for running water. That happened awfully quick. She wouldn't have made it outside in time.

Neil stepped in from doing chores. "What's the matter? Are you all right?"

Anna rubbed her stomach. "I must have a touch of the flu."

By afternoon, she felt better. *Just a twelve-hour bug.*

But the next morning, it happened again, then yet again. She covered her mouth with her hands as the realization hit. *Oh my... it couldn't be...* She wasn't pregnant again, was she? She hadn't been so sick with Kevin, and she'd forgotten about her morning sickness with Monica.

When Neil came in for breakfast, she blurted out, "I think I'm pregnant. I'd better go see the doctor."

A huge grin lit up his face. "Aha. That's why you've been sick these last few mornings." He swept her up in a bear hug. "Oh, my little mama."

Anna tried to feel celebratory with him, but she couldn't quite muster up the happy energy. She'd thought she was done having babies. With a three-year-old still toddling around, how would she find the time and energy to take care of a newborn? She shook aside the negative thoughts. Monica was nine—she would help.

In Foster, Doc Farnum confirmed her diagnosis. "Yes, indeed, you're going to have another little one." He smiled. "See, just a few short years ago, you were worried that you wouldn't have a big family."

Anna knew she should feel happy that she was able to give Neil another child. It was fashionable to have large families. She had heard the neighbor women gossip about a childless couple, "Must be something wrong with her." Or about the family with only one or two children, "Wonder if she can't have any more?"

But she felt so sick. And she was already tired, taking care of Monica and Kevin and trying to help Neil outside as much as possible. It would mean another summer she wouldn't be able to drive tractor for him. Unlike some of the other neighborhood wives, she enjoyed being outside, gardening and doing farm work—she was with her partner and best friend in life, and they were accomplishing something, together.

As the summer went by, she found she could do less and less without feeling totally exhausted. She was tired all the time, and she felt so cumbersome. "I need a wheelbarrow to carry my stomach around in," she remarked to Neil.

He laughed and hugged her. "Just relax, little mother. Take advantage of your condition, sit down and rest for a change."

The doctor agreed when she went in for her regular checkup.

At the end of July, beginning her seventh month, her legs and feet suddenly grew puffy, she was short of breath, dizzy, and even more tired. Anna had a nagging feeling that something was wrong. Finally, one morning she told Neil, "I don't think the baby is moving around as much as it was."

Neil immediately bundled her and the two kids into the car and drove to Foster to see Doc Farnum.

The doctor discarded his pipe and shook his head when he read her blood pressure. "Pretty high, there, young lady. Better draw some blood." He poked and prodded.

Anna yawned. Too many questions. Why didn't he just get this over with so she go home and sleep?

"Well, dear, I'm afraid we've got a case of toxemia here. It's rare that it happens with anything but a first baby, but once in a great while…" Doc peered at Anna and Neil from beneath his bushy white eyebrows. "We'd better send her in to Miles City today. She may need an emergency Cesarean section right away."

Anna gasped. "*Ach, nein.* It's too early, it's too early," she whispered over and over. "Where are the kids? What are we going to do…?" Her head spun. Chills raced up her spine.

"I saw Gertie Sparks come into the waiting room." Neil smoothed her hair. "I'll ask her to take the kids. And I'll call the Jersey Lily, get a message to Mom and Dad."

The ambulance howled its way over the narrow, eighty-mile highway to Miles City. Anna lay in the back, clutching Neil's hand, as the technician monitored her blood pressure. *Toxemia.*

Surgery. Her throat constricted, her heart pounded. She wanted to cry, to scream the clawing fear right out of her. Would she lose the baby? *Ach du lieber. This can't be happening. Mutti—I want my Mutti.*

They arrived with a squeal of brakes at the emergency room door, and nurses whisked her away.

Anna was surrounded by figures in white. Someone placed a mask over her nose and mouth. "Count backwards from one hundred," came the instruction, as she felt a needle prick in her abdomen.

"One hundred, ninety-nine, ninety-eight…" White clouds whirled around Anna's head, and she floated. Fleetingly, she wondered if she was dying and if this was heaven. She heard voices droning from far away. She drifted… so peaceful… Then a sudden stab of pain as the knife slashed across her belly. She screamed.

"Not enough anesthesia," yelled the doctor. "More."

"I swear I gave her enough," retorted the anesthesiologist. "What's wrong?"

"She can feel every move I make here."

"It's too late. I can't give her any more at this point; it would harm the baby."

Ach, lieber Gott. I'm being killed… The pain became a living thing, stabbing and thrusting its sword through her belly. Anna screamed again. *Oh please stop. I want to die.* The room grew dim and darkness mercifully enveloped her.

~~~

The bright lights in the waiting room seared Neil's eyes. He shivered in the cold-green room and scrubbed his hands through his hair. He'd never felt more alone.

Then Anna screamed. He leaped from his chair and ran toward the operating room door.

"No. I'm sorry, Mr. Moser, you can't go in there." The burly nurse flung her body across the opening.

"What are they doing? Why is she screaming?" Frantic, Neil clenched his fists and paced furiously in front of the door.

"Just wait here, Mr. Moser, I'll go find out what's happening." The nurse spoke in a calm voice, but it failed to soothe him. He continued to pace, stopping to pound his fists against his thighs.

A few minutes later, the head nurse came bustling through the door. "Mr. Moser, I'm sorry for your discomfort. Apparently the anesthesia didn't take full effect, and she could feel the surgery. Everything is fine. Don't worry. The procedure is progressing normally." With those empty platitudes, she was gone.

No! This is not normal. Neil collapsed into the chair, his head in his hands. What was happening? Would he lose his beloved Anna this time? And the baby? He had worried the last two times she was in childbirth, but then everything was normal. Something had gone wrong this time. "Dear God…" The tears came, and he wept and prayed as never before.

CHAPTER TWO

A gentle touch on his shoulder brought him back. The doctor pulled the mask from his face and sat down next to him. "Mr. Moser, your wife and daughter are doing fine. Five pounds, three ounces."

Neil's hands shook. He was lightheaded with relief. "Oh, Doc," he gasped. "What...? They're okay?"

"Mrs. Moser will be under a little while longer, but the baby is in the nursery, if you'd like to see her."

"Oh. Oh, yes. Yes, I do." He stood and nearly staggered as he moved toward the viewing window. The nursery was painted a cheery yellow, with baby ducks and chicks, kittens and puppies stenciled on the walls. In front of the window stood a row of bassinets, blue and pink blankets covering the babies.

Neil gazed through the glass at his new daughter—so tiny compared to the others—lying in the incubator just behind the bassinets, a pink knitted cap on her head. Red, wrinkled skin, little fists waving frantically, she opened her mouth wide as if to roar her protest at this new world. He grinned. *She may be small, but she sure has a big voice.*

"Well, Elizabeth Moser, you certainly came into the world with a bang," Neil whispered.

Later, when Anna awakened and was able to nurse the baby, Neil went in to see them. His heart aching with love, he smiled at his wife, who'd gone through so much to give him another child. Her face was pale, her bloodshot eyes had dark circles and her hair was matted and damp, but to him she was the most beautiful woman in the world. "Thank you. I'm so proud of you."

Anna shifted in bed and grimaced. "I really thought I was going to die." She shook her head. "Having a big family isn't worth all this. No more babies. Never again."

No sooner had Anna's head hit the pillow her first night home when Elizabeth squalled as though in pain. Anna bolted upright, grimacing in pain from the incision. She rose gingerly, went to the crib next to her bed, and picked up Elizabeth. Her little face wrinkled and red with anger, she continued her raucous lament. After changing the baby's diaper, Anna walked around the living room, into the kitchen and back again. She sang to her, jiggled her and changed positions. She sat in the rocking chair to feed her, but little Elizabeth was having none of it. She was colicky, she was mad at the world, and nothing Anna could do would change that. It was almost as if Elizabeth knew she'd had a traumatic entrance to life.

Night after night, for months, this continued. Because of her need to heal from the C-section, Neil spelled her often, which meant they were both exhausted. Anna thought she had surely walked to North Dakota and back by now. Or at least worn a path in the living room rug. Some nights she swore she must have been sleepwalking, because she lost track of time and what she was doing. None of the family could get a good night's rest. It was hard to get nine-year-old Monica up in the morning for school, and she yawned over her breakfast. Kevin, at three, was up early anyway and played quietly with his tractors and trucks.

When they took her to the doctor, he merely shook his head. "We don't know why some babies are so fussy. There's really nothing wrong with her that I can see." He puffed on his pipe. "It won't last forever."

Anna's shoulders slumped wearily. *It already seems like a lifetime. I don't know if I can go through much more of this.*

Finally, after three months, Elizabeth seemed to grow out of her colicky stage and only awoke a few times. "I'm almost afraid to say anything, but Lizzie slept almost all the way through last night," Anna told Neil one morning.

But that night the screams started again. More walking, more comforting, more getting up. Anna came to understand what the phrase "at the end of my rope" meant. Even though Neil helped her walk and jiggle and sing to the baby, it seemed as though Anna was all alone in this battle. A dark, heavy cloud hovered over her.

~~~

And so it went through Lizzie's first two years, when Anna learned what the phrase "terrible twos" really meant.

She couldn't turn her back for a second. Lizzie was in the lower cupboards, throwing out all the pots and pans. Anna had to move breakable things way up out of reach, something she hadn't worried much about with the other two. And she could have sworn Lizzie's first word was "NO!"

"Why can't you be more like your big sister?" she burst out in exasperation, regretting her words immediately. Most of her time was consumed by her third child, and the rest of the family often had to fend for themselves. Monica was a big help, but guilt plagued Anna that she relied on her oldest for so much.

She would often stop and lean her head against the wall during one of Lizzie's tantrums. *I wish Mutti was here.* Anna had no one to talk to about raising a difficult child. Nettie was no help, living fifty miles away. And when she and Jake did come to visit, her mother-in-law studiously avoided interaction with Lizzie. Anna gritted her teeth. *Doesn't she like this baby?* She and her mother-in-law had gone through some rough times in the early years, but Anna had thought their relationship had improved. Her shoulders slumped. *I wish I could talk to her about these problems I'm having.*

There was no one in the neighborhood in which to confide. It would only become the topic of neighborhood gossip on the new party-line phone system. It was none of their business anyway. She could hardly wait till Lizzie was old enough to send to school.

~~~

"M-o-m." Monica called from the kitchen. "Come check this."

Anna covered Lizzie with her blanket and tiptoed out of the bedroom, hoping she would stay asleep for a few minutes. Thirteen-year-old Monica was laying out pattern pieces on blue cotton yardage for her 4-H project.

"I got it all pinned, and I started to cut it out, but you better check it."

Anna looked at the pieces. She took in a sharp breath. "Oh, no, honey. This has to go with the straight grain of fabric. See the arrow? Oh, dear, you've already cut this one out. And I don't think you have enough material left to re-pin it."

Monica's face fell. She stared at the work she had done and threw down the scissors. "I never can do anything right." She turned and stomped out of the house, letting the screen door slam. Anna cringed, waiting for Lizzie's yell. Sure enough, it came. Anna took a step toward the door, torn, wishing she could follow Monica, but knowing she couldn't leave the four-year-old alone. She sighed and went back to the bedroom.

"I want my bottle."

"No, honey. Remember, you're a *big* girl now, and big girls don't drink bottles." Anna had given in and let her have the bottle much too long, and now she was paying the price. She rocked her youngest, trying to get her to go back to sleep. She sighed, wishing she could talk to Monica. She didn't think she'd spoken in a critical way. Where had she gone wrong? She just wanted to teach her daughter to do good work. "When you do something, do it right," Papa had always told her. It seemed good enough advice to pass on to her kids. Oh, why couldn't she just pick up the telephone and talk to Mutti? But the phone line barely worked even in the neighborhood, and everyone listened in on the party line to every call.

Nothing seemed to be going right with Monica. She had become moody, given to bouts of tears and anger over the least little thing, sometimes refusing to talk for days. Anna's pubescent daughter was dissatisfied with her looks, her lot, her life. A growth spurt had taken her to an unlikely five-foot-eight at age twelve, and she towered over everyone in school, including the teacher. Now, at thirteen, she was all-too-soon past her tomboy stage and constantly stared into the mirror, moaning about her naturally curly hair. "Why can't I get it to flip up straight, like these pictures in the magazines?"

Neil was no help with their daughter. Oh, he tried. Anna knew he wanted to help, but he only seemed to get in the way. So he vanished as soon as Anna and Monica started a project together. "Don't know anything about woman stuff," he'd mutter on his way out the door.

And Kevin… School was a trial for him. The teacher hired three years ago when Kevin started first grade, Mr. Quail, was a highly intelligent, world-traveled, well-educated person, with whom she and Neil passed many a pleasant evening in conversation. They had eagerly entered discussions about Castro seizing power in Cuba, rehashed the Kennedy-Nixon debates, and lamented the huge balance of payments deficit—a record $3.7 billion in 1959. It had been refreshing to be able to talk about world events, or music and philosophy, rather than just about the weather and the cows.

But Mr. Quail had been a tyrant of a teacher. The four little first-graders sat wide-eyed in terror as his booming voice pronounced the rules. The little neighbor boy, Douglas Edwards, wet his pants nearly every day, and Kevin often complained of a stomachache and begged to stay home from school. He was happier following his daddy around and helping "fix" the machinery.

Last year, chubby Mr. Sunderland had been a breath of fresh air—young, pleasant, and cheerful. But, of course, he didn't want to stay another year. "Sorry," he'd said. "I have an offer from a bigger school." A one-room country school a hundred miles from a sizable town was not a big draw for good teachers.

The applications they received were either from recent graduates with no experience, or "has-beens" who couldn't get a job anywhere else. There had already been a rift in the neighborhood over teachers. Neil had been on the school board that had hired Mr. Quail, and the Edwardses were no longer speaking to the Mosers.

This year, Mrs. Nelson was a sweet, grandmotherly type, excellent with the littlest kids, but ineffectual with upper grades. As an eighth-grader, Monica practically taught herself, and tutored the rest of the kids, too. She had even been drafted to roll up Mrs. Nelson's hair during recess on Friday afternoons.

Anna sighed, thinking of next year when Monica would enter high school. For that, her little girl would have to live in a dormitory thirty-five miles away.

And this 4-H business. Hmmph. She shook her head and gently lay Lizzie back down on her bed. First off, the local club's sewing "leader," Mrs. Mitchell, didn't even know how to sew, so all the girls came to Anna for help. Well, at least she had mastered the art of sewing, after a rocky start. Her mouth curled in a wry smile, remembering the tiff she and Nettie had when she first tried to learn.

Then, Monica had worked so hard all summer, making a green wool suit for the fair and to enter the "Make it With Wool Contest." She had done a beautiful job, and had won a blue ribbon. Anna's heart overflowed with pride.

"Well, of course, her mother did it for her." Anna had overheard Mrs. Mitchell talking to someone outside the door of the 4-H building during the fair. "That's why she gets such good grades in school, too. Her parents do everything for her."

Anna had tasted blood as she bit her lip, and she bent over, pounding her fists against her thighs to keep herself from going out there and giving that woman a piece of her mind.

Now, she wished she had. How could people be so cruel? She went to the kitchen and stared at the blue fabric covering the table. It would be a challenge, but she needed to teach her daughter not to feel sorry for herself, to be proud of her accomplishments, despite what others might say.

There weren't any other girls Monica's age within thirty-five miles, even in the 4-H club. Would her daughter be able to learn social skills? *Mine aren't that great either.*

The shy girl longed for a friend, "somebody my own age, Mom."

She tried to encourage the teen. "You'll have lots of friends when you go to high school, honey, you'll see."

Anna sure could use a friend to talk to. Her kind-hearted neighbor Vicki Thompson had moved away eight years ago because there hadn't been a school for her son to attend. Gertie, the woman from Germany, lived so far away, and the other neighbor women were so gossipy and always seemed too busy with their big families.

She drew a deep breath. Maybe she should go visit with Gertie. The woman's no-nonsense, down-to-earth attitude might be just the thing she needed.

~~~

As Neil headed toward the house, he heard the door slam and Monica's raised voice,

"...never do anything right!"

Uh-oh, they were at it again. Abruptly, he planted the heel of his work boot in the dusty soil and did an about-face, heading back to the shop. The old Case tractor still needed a lot of work....

He didn't know how to deal with two females always at war with each other. All he knew was that he didn't want to be in the middle of it. They'd been sewing again. He shook his head, remembering when his mother had tried to help Anna learn to sew. Hadn't Anna stalked off into the bedroom, reduced to tears because she felt like she couldn't do things right for Nettie? In a lot of ways, being a man was so much simpler. Neil picked up his wrench, and disappeared under the tractor.

~~~

Anna stirred the pot of stew, then turned toward the sound of the kitchen door opening. Monica slunk in, her head down, eyes averted.

"Hi. Supper's almost ready. Would you go find Daddy and Kevin and tell them to come in." As the teenager turned to go back out, Anna squared her shoulders. She couldn't let this sewing thing loom between them. She took a deep breath. "Listen, honey, I think the blue dress will work out fine. You'll see, the difference in grain on the front bodice won't show that much. You can wear it to school."

Monica raised her chin, her blue eyes shiny. "Okay, Mom. I'll go out and yell for Dad and Kevin, then I'll set the table."

Anna's shoulders relaxed and she breathed easier.

Before her daughter reached the door, Neil flung it open and strode in, carrying Kevin. Kevin's pant leg was ripped open from knee to ankle and covered with blood.

Anna froze, the world tilted around her and gradually faded into soft-focus. All her nurse's training, all the gore of the war wounds she'd seen had not prepared her for the sight of her own son covered in blood.

Her hands clutched her chest. "*Ach du lieber.* What happened?"

"Mom, I cut myself a little bit." To her surprise, he wasn't crying. Anna frowned at Neil. Hadn't he been paying attention?

Her husband seemed to read her mind. "He was playing around that old machinery up on the hill while I worked on the tractor."

She grabbed the nearest thing available, the dishtowel, slid to the floor beside him and with shaking hands dabbed at the wound on the inside of the calf—a gaping three-inch-long gash, almost to the bone. Images of war injuries flashed through her mind. She swallowed bile. "Monica, get me a basin of water."

Lizzie appeared from the bedroom. "That's ugly." But she stood watching, transfixed.

Anna washed the cut and applied pressure. The bleeding wouldn't stop. She lifted her gaze to Neil and saw her anguish mirrored on his face. "We'd better get him to the doctor." She tried to tape the gash shut the best she could, folded several thick towels over it, and tied them tight. Neil carried their son to the car, Anna running to keep up with his long strides. She called over her shoulder, "Monica, take care of Lizzie. Please eat something. We'll be back soon."

In the back seat with Kevin, she kept compression on the leg. "The bleeding seems to be lessening." She allowed herself to lean back against the seat. "It's going to be okay." She smoothed the damp hair from Kevin's forehead.

Neil shot her a look over his shoulder and nodded. "Good."

A tetanus shot and numerous stitches later, they were on their way home again. She looked at her son's pale face, and breathed a huge sigh of relief. Life seemed to be just one crisis after another. Would things even out, get easier as the kids got older? Trying to raise a family so far from doctors, schools, even other kids… It was a monumental task. In spite of her own challenges in the war, her life in Germany had not prepared her for the hardships of rural Montana.

She heaved a ragged breath. At times she felt wholly inadequate to be a mother. *Lord, I need a lot of help.*

~~~

A few days later, Anna called Gertie Sparks. She needed to hear her mother tongue. They met for coffee in Foster, a half-way point for both.

"So, *wie gehts?*" Gertie bubbled as she slipped into the booth at the café.

"*Gut.*" Anna drew a deep breath. Did she dare confide in someone who was not family? "Well... life in Montana sure is different from back home." She spoke in German, slipping comfortably back into her mother tongue. *Ah, I needed this.*

Gertie laughed and lit a cigarette. "Ja, it sure is."

Anna related Kevin's accident and then told her about Monica, the gossip about her sewing, and how the neighbors seemed so critical of Anna and her family. "I don't know what I ever did to anyone to make them not like me. How do you deal with it?"

"Ach, pshaw." Gertie blew out a ring of smoke. "*Macht nichts.* It don't matter what they think. I don't give a damn, and you shouldn't either. Hell, they laughed at me behind my back in *Deutschland* too. I had to go to work in a pub so I wouldn't starve, and they called me *eine Hure.*"

Anna gave a little gasp at Gertie's coarse language. *Oh dear. Life was much rougher for her then.* "*Ach du lieber,* I'm so sorry..."

"You don't need to be sorry. You didn't call me those names." The woman shook her head. "I'm just telling you, don't worry about what other people think. It's not worth a hill o' beans. And it don't hurt nobody but yourself."

Driving home, Anna replayed their conversation over and over. Maybe Gertie had a point. Could she become that thick-skinned? *But do I want to?*

CHAPTER THREE

Cool spring air wafted through the open window. Neil had just crawled into bed with Anna after an evening of wrangling with Lizzie and Kevin, trying to get them to settle down. "Read me another story." ... "I'm thirsty." ... "Lay with me awhile."... Bedtime was such a madhouse, and it seemed to be getting worse all the time. But finally the house had settled in for the night, its creaks and groans gradually subsiding with the gentle snoring of its inhabitants.

Neil bolted upright from a deep sleep as he heard the front door crash open. Someone called out, "Hello? Neil? Anna? Hello?"

"It's Dad!" Neil slid out of bed and into his pants. He looked at the clock by the bed. One a.m. "What in the world?"

He loped out to the kitchen, Anna hurrying behind, shrugging into her pink chenille bathrobe. Jake and Neil's cousin, Marilyn, stood in the middle of the room. Tears streamed down Jake's face.

"It's your mother... I couldn't tell you over the phone... She... she..." His normally strong voice broke, and he groped for a chair.

"Mom?" Neil stopped in mid-step. Ice ran through his veins. "What happened?"

"One minute she was standing there, talking and laughing, and the next..." Jake couldn't go on.

Marilyn stepped forward and put a warm hand on Neil's chilled arm. Her soft, calm voice competed with the pounding of

21

his heart. "It happened earlier this evening, right after supper. The doctor said it was a brain aneurysm. She went instantly."

"Oh, dear God, no." Neil choked. "I can't believe it." He turned and reached for Anna, still standing with her hands to her mouth. His tears came as she embraced him.

They all stood in the kitchen with their arms around one another for what seemed like hours, letting the terrible news sink in. Neil glanced over his dad's shoulder. Monica stood in the doorway, clutching and unclutching the hem of her robe, a stricken look on her face. And Lizzie just behind her. But he couldn't move. His body was frozen, his feet leaden. How could he comfort them?

Anna extricated herself gently and went to the girls. "Gramma died tonight, honey." The teenager nodded, her blue eyes a stark contrast to her white face. Lizzie just kept staring, wide-eyed at the sad little group

Neil slumped into a kitchen chair. This was all just a nightmare, wasn't it? It couldn't be true.

Anna made coffee, and they talked about funeral arrangements. Jake and Nettie had retired a couple of years earlier and moved to Billings to be near Nettie's sister, Margie Tester, and her daughter, Marilyn and her family.

"We'd better all go to town today and get things settled," Anna said finally. "Let me fix some breakfast; then we can go."

Neil nodded, too numb to even think.

~~~

Anna tossed and turned, alone in a strange bed at Marilyn's house. Neil had gone to stay with Jake at the trailer. He had hardly said a word the whole trip to town. This was the first time she had ever seen him break down and cry. What a helpless feeling. She didn't know what to do. There was no way to comfort him, no way to break through the barrier that he'd suddenly thrown up. It was as though she were on the outside of a glass wall, looking in at Neil, only he couldn't see her standing out there.

Nettie wasn't yet fifty-eight years old. An incredible wave of sadness washed over her and a hot tear oozed from under her closed lids to splash on the pillow. Now Nettie wouldn't get to see her grandchildren grow up. Sure, she and her mother-in-law had had their differences. They'd never quite accepted each other and had never become totally comfortable in each other's company. But she still had hoped there would be time for them to do that. Anna missed her own Mutti so much.

She stared at the darkness. *But Nettie has a good heart; she loves her son. She sure is good to the grandkids. Monica adores her and she is... was... family...*

Anna turned onto her back. That was another thing that bothered her—Monica had not yet cried. That girl was much too contained, too serious, too quiet. But she didn't know how to draw out her daughter. She was so much like her dad, a very deep well, the bottom kept just out of sight.

~~~

Neil lay on the fold-out couch at his dad's trailer. He breathed in the lingering scent of his mother's face powder. An icy tendril of sorrow clutched at his heart. She was gone. His mother was gone... dead. He'd never known a day without his mom. His body felt like a hollow shell. He lay there, numbness overcoming him, as the tears welled up, yet again.

~~~

Nettie's sister, Margie Tester's house hummed with activity. Anna watched from the sidelines. Relatives from all over the state had arrived—Nettie's sisters and their families—cousins, aunts, and the bachelor uncles everyone still called "the boys." Covered dishes of food filled the kitchen counters. Kids shouted and chased each other in the yard. The adults clustered together in tight little knots, speaking in hushed voices.

That afternoon Neil and Anna drove Jake and Monica to the funeral home. A solemn-faced man in a black suit ushered the family into a small room off to the side of the lectern. This would be Monica's first funeral. Anna wanted to shield her daughter against this heartache of death and loss. *I hope it was the right decision to bring her.* They'd left Kevin and Lizzie at home with the neighbors.

She watched the rest of the church fill—women dressed in black, wearing hats with little black fishnet veils over their faces, men shuffling behind, removing their hats and holding them over their chests as they waited to be seated. The organ moaned, and women sniffed behind dainty lace hankies. Anna sneaked a sideways glance at Neil and Jake. They sat stiffly, staring straight ahead. Her own face felt like it was made of stone.

The minister began the eulogy. He talked about Nettie as though he'd known her, how she had loved horses and ranch work. She rolled her eyes. He had never even met her. But what he said was true—how did he know that?

A sob burst from Monica, and she buried her face in a handkerchief. Anna scooted a little closer and put an arm around her daughter's shaking shoulders, dabbing at her own tears. *Good. It's good to let it out.* With her other hand, she took Neil's and held tight to both her husband and her daughter.

~~~

Back home a couple of days later, Anna scoured the kitchen sink, even though it still shone from yesterday's cleaning. Death was so final. "*Ja, ja,* I know, Lord, I believe in life ever after, but…" Her eyes lifted as if in apology. But it was excruciating for those left behind.

Jake had looked so forlorn when they left him at his trailer in Billings the day after the funeral. Monica spent hours walking in the spring-greened hills these days, probably avoiding the stony silence around home. Anna had thought the tears at the funeral were a break-through, but now her daughter had clammed up again. Kevin and Lizzie had been staying with the neighbors for the past week, so Anna didn't even have their raucous play and laughter for distraction.

She grabbed the broom and stabbed it into the corners. Back home, the Catholics had their wake, and then seemed to forget about it. *Okay, fine, I can do that, if that's what supposed to be done.* Her mouth pressed into a thin line. But Neil. There was no talking to him. He was unreachable, behind that glass wall, as if he thought himself invisible. She had no idea how to help him with his grief.

"Nope, I'm fine," was his answer when she asked him if he was having a hard time.

"Nothin' to talk about," when she pressed him for his feelings.

She wiped her eyes. *Sure, but the rest of your family is sad and lonely too,* she wanted to say to him. *They're important too.*

She supposed their stoic European ancestry kept her husband and daughter so quiet, so inside themselves. As long as they didn't talk about things, the problems didn't exist. As long as they didn't think about them, they wouldn't have to deal with them, either. She caught her breath. *Maybe that's what I'm doing too—holding it all in.*

~ ~ ~

Neil upended the oilcan into the tractor's engine. Time to start it up and see how his overhaul job worked. He hoped he hadn't left out something important. In his head, he ticked off the steps. Nope, should be ready to go. Now, if everything worked right...

"Neil. Dinner's ready."

He sighed. He didn't really want to go in and sit through dinner, enduring his wife's probing stares. A coil of pain rose up from his stomach and wrapped itself around his chest. He stopped, bent his head toward his knees and tried to breathe deeply. Anna wanted to talk about death. Well, it wasn't exactly a pleasant subject. He'd rather not get into it. His mother was in a better place—he knew that—but... "Lord, how I miss her." The words burst from his throat in an anguished cry and surprised him. He couldn't stand the pain. "No, no, no." Clunking down

25

the oilcan, he grabbed a rag and rubbed at his hands. He couldn't deal with it.

Pushing thoughts of his mother aside, he headed for the house.

The silence hit Neil like a wave as he entered the kitchen. Dinner was on the table. Anna and Monica already sat in their places, waiting. He ran the water in the sink until it was hot. He had experienced anguish, even anger at times, because Anna and Nettie hadn't gotten along. Now his mother was gone, but he still had his wife and family. He had to think about life with them again. The tight coil in his chest eased a bit.

"Let's bring Kevin and Lizzie home tonight." He scrubbed the grease from his fingers. "It seems awful quiet around here without them."

CHAPTER FOUR

"I'm so glad you'll be rooming with Lila; at least she's somebody you know." Anna turned her head toward Monica sitting in the back seat of their new beige Chevy Bel Air. "And you have all those new clothes you made last summer. You look so pretty."

Monica's eyes remained downcast. She didn't answer.

Anna chattered to fill the silence as they drove toward Foster, taking Monica to her first day of high school. Somehow they'd all made it through the summer without talking much about Nettie's death. They'd tucked the subject into the background like a discarded item packed away in an unused room, the door firmly shut.

She glanced into the back seat. How pretty her daughter looked, dressed in the bright red corduroy jumper Monica had made, her blonde hair curled under at her shoulders. Her suitcase was packed for the week's stay in the dorm, and she had a brand new notebook and pencil case filled with new pens and pencils. But even though Monica hadn't said anything, Anna sensed her nervousness.

Heavens, she was terrified herself. Now everything was out of her control; Monica was leaving the nest. Everything was going to be new—the school, the teachers, the kids, sharing a room in the dorm, being away from home all week... boys. Would the kids in high school make fun of her daughter because Anna was German? She shuddered. Well, at least Lila would take Monica under her wing. She was a senior, very down-to-earth and sensible. And the third roommate, Sally, was a sophomore, another no-nonsense country girl. At least she could be somewhat content that they wouldn't lead her little girl astray.

27

Anna was glad they'd already met the dorm matron and checked out the room the girls would share on the second floor, boys on the first. She was certain Mrs. Dirning ruled with a firm hand.

"With 150 kids in school, just think of all the new friends you'll meet. Aren't you excited?"

"Yeah, Mom, I'm excited," Monica muttered in a monotone.

Anna smiled brightly, holding back a sob that threatened to slide up her throat. Her daughter was like Neil. She withdrew when she was nervous, frightened, or threatened with emotion.

"You'll be just fine, honey." She reached back to squeeze Monica's arm. "There's a phone in the dorm; call us every night if you want to. School will be a breeze—you're a smart girl, and you'll get acquainted soon. You already know Lila and Sally and Carla, and there's a bunch of girls you met through 4-H."

Neil turned on the blinker to signal their turn onto the gravel street leading to the school. The end of summer clung to September with shimmery waves of heat as a little dust devil picked up a stray tumbleweed and blew it across the road. Neil braked to a stop in front of the gray two-story, brick-sided dormitory. He got out, stretched and reached into the trunk for Monica's suitcase.

"Well, the second generation of Mosers has arrived." He looked up at the two-story building. "This is where I lived during my senior year of high school. My room was the third from the end. We had some good times…" Pointing at the window he smiled, and draped an arm around his daughter's shoulders. "You will, too."

"I'd better get going. Gotta get unpacked and find my first classroom." Monica withdrew from her dad's embrace, gave Anna a quick peck on the cheek, picked up her suitcase and started up the steps. She turned and waved. "'Bye, Mom, Dad. See you Friday."

Anna crumpled a hanky in her fist and held it to her mouth as they got back into the car. "*Ach, du lieber,* our little girl leaving home. I can't believe it." She turned to Neil, noting an unusual shininess in his eyes. Sliding closer to him on the seat, she leaned her head against his shoulder. "And tomorrow our other little girl starts kindergarten already. It seems like only yesterday when she was born... both of them... all of them." Kevin was almost ten and in the fourth grade.

Time traveled faster than the road slipping beneath them. She had celebrated her fortieth birthday last February. Forty years old. "Old," that was the word. She had been in America almost sixteen years already, and had been home to visit only once. Her own parents were getting up in their sixties now, and she missed them. Her big family in Germany always found some excuse for a get-together, with lots of food, beer, and wine, singing, laughing and joking. Here, she and Neil were the only ones in the neighborhood who didn't have an extended family to invite or to go visit for holidays. Their Thanksgivings and Christmases had always been small gatherings, quiet and relaxed, with Jake and Nettie, and now... only Jake. A sudden longing overcame her.

Anna hugged herself and blinked back tears. She missed her sister and cousins, sharing secrets, joys and fears. She still didn't have a woman friend here she could really talk to.

Gertie Sparks came to visit now and again, and they reminisced about home, but that was about the extent of their camaraderie. Other than their birth country, they had little in common.

Of course there *was* Evelyn Gharrett. She, her husband, Bud, and their eleven-year-old daughter, Lana, had recently moved onto the Wicker place about twenty miles away. Anna felt a small ping of hope. They seemed like nice folks. But Evelyn had a knack of calling when Anna was busy, wanting to stop by and visit in the middle of the afternoon. Anna frowned. She didn't have time for that kind of thing. Then she shook her head. *But if you don't make the time, you'll never have a friend.* When had she become so reclusive?

"So what are we going to do without our helper?" Neil's question broke into her reverie.

She sighed. "I don't know. Monica is such a good girl, always taking care of the little ones, and helping both of us with chores. Oh, Kevin loves to help you outside, but Lizzie... I can't even get her to make her own bed in the morning. I just don't know what to do with her sometimes."

"I hope she'll be okay, being away from home—Monica, I mean." Neil reached out for Anna's hand. "She's so shy. I hope she doesn't get homesick. It wasn't so bad for me when I came to the dorm. I'd already been boarding out most of my school years."

Anna's throat tightened. *Oh, dear Lord, I do hope she'll be all right.*

~~~

Kevin came to breakfast, dressed in his new blue denims and a navy plaid shirt, his dark hair wet down and slicked to the side. "I can't wait to meet the new teacher, Mom. Dougie said he met her already, and she's really, really nice."

Anna kissed his forehead. Her sensitive little man. She hoped he would have a good year in school, without his older sister there to protect him from the bigger kids' bullying. She dished up a bowl of oatmeal, sprinkled on raisins and brown sugar and poured milk over it.

"Lizzie, come for breakfast." Nothing but silence.

"I think she went back to bed." Kevin dug into his cereal.

Anna bustled into the bedroom. Sure enough, the covers were pulled up over the small body, just a tousled mop of brown curls sticking out. "Come on, honey, you've got to go to school." She pulled the quilt off. Lizzie lay there grinning. She was dressed in her oldest, dirtiest play clothes, the ones with holes and patches all over.

"Elizabeth!" Anna turned to the closet and grabbed the hanger with the new pussy willow print dress. "You were going to wear your new dress for the first day of school, remember?"

"No."

"Why not?" Anna put her hands in her apron pockets to keep from slapping her daughter.

"Cuz…" Lizzie looked up with a coquettish pout. "Cuz I'm not goin' t' school."

Anna threw up her hands. What brought this about? Lizzie had been excited to go to school. She loved playing with other kids, and she always wanted to go wherever Kevin went. Anna sat down on the edge of the bed. "Now, honey. We've talked about this. You're five years old, and when big girls are five, they get to go to kindergarten. The teacher started a special class for you and Bonnie. You don't want her to get ahead of you, do you?"

"I don't care." Lizzie pulled the blanket up to her chin again.

Anna bit the inside of her cheek and held her breath, letting it out very slowly. God had certainly blessed her with a willful child. She sometimes wished she had just had two children. Oh no, what was she thinking? She shook her head abruptly to chase away the thought.

"All right, Miss Elizabeth Annette Moser, you get up out of that bed and get that dress on right now, or you'll be getting a spanking." She turned on her heel and marched out of the room, shaking with frustration.

A few minutes later, a little lady came prancing into the kitchen, wearing her new dress—and old rotted-out tennis shoes. Anna rolled her eyes. "Here's your breakfast." She wasn't up to fighting any more battles this morning.

~~~

After school, her two young ones came running into the house, chattering and giggling.

"Mom, Mom! I like school," Lizzie yelled at the top of her lungs. Her new dress was smudged and wrinkled and hung limp from her shoulders.

Kevin tossed his lunchbox on the counter. "Mrs. Bradley is really neat, Mom. She read to us after lunch, and she's teaching us to play football at recess, and... can we have some cookies?"

Anna gave them each a glass of milk and an oatmeal-raisin cookie.

"Lizzie was naughty at school, though."

Her daughter straightened defiantly and cocked her head. "Was not."

"Were too." Kevin scrunched his face into a serious expression. "Mom, she got out of her seat and went running around the room and knocked over Mrs. Bradley's cup of coffee."

"Tattletale." Lizzie stuck out her tongue.

"Kids. Now stop. Kevin, I'm sure Mrs. Bradley will handle Lizzie just fine. Lizzie, you do what your teacher tells you. And you must stay in your seat during class. It's only three more days until Friday. If you're good, we'll take you both with us when we go pick up your big sister in Foster." Anna put the milk back in the refrigerator. *Is every day going to be a fight with Lizzie?*

~ ~ ~

Kevin and Lizzie bounced and sang in the back seat as Neil drove them all to Foster to pick up Monica.

"When're we gonna get there?"

"Will she 'member us?"

"Of course she will. It's only been a week." Anna felt like bouncing too. "I can't wait to see her, either."

They all sat in the car by the dorm, windows rolled down, waiting for the high school across the street to disgorge its crop of students for the week.

"There she is," shouted Kevin.

Anna saw her, wearing a pink skirt and blouse, tall and slender, walking with her roommates, Lila and Sally. When Monica spotted the car, her face lit up with a big smile. She peeled away from her friends and ran to them. "Hi, Mom, Dad. Hiya,

Brats, how ya doin'?" She rumpled their hair through the car window. "I gotta get my suitcase. Want to come up and see our room, Mom? Sorry, Dad, only girls allowed on the second floor."

"I wanna go, too," Lizzie whined.

"Okay. But stay close to me." Anna grabbed her by the hand.

The dorm was a hubbub of activity. Boys and girls shouting good-byes, carrying duffel bags and suitcases out to their cars—if they were lucky enough to have one of their own—or meeting their parents who'd come to pick them up. Somewhere, a radio was playing, blasting out that new rock group, the Beatles' "I Want to Hold Your Hand."

They climbed the stairs to the second floor, Anna hanging tight to Lizzie to keep her from running off to explore. Monica opened the door to her room, where Lila and Sally were doing some last-minute packing. The three girls shared the smallest room in the dorm, where a door led outside to the fire escape.

"Well, I guess Mrs. Dirning trusts you girls not to use that door to sneak out late at night," Anna teased.

Lila giggled. "Yeah, she knows we're all wallflowers."

Anna glanced around the room, at the posters, the bunkbeds crowded against the wall, a study table under the window, the tiny closet.

"How do you girls get around in here without bumping into each other?"

"Oh, it's a good thing we're friends." Sally stuffed clothes into her suitcase. "The dorm is really full this year—sixty kids. So almost every room has three in it. Luckily we have a big bathroom with lots of mirrors just down the hall."

Monica grabbed her suitcase. "Okay, Mom, I'm ready. I gotta sign out before I leave."

On the way home, Monica filled her family in on life in town. "We go uptown to the drugstore for Cokes after school almost every day. It's fun. And Wednesday night we went to see the new Elvis movie, "Kissin' Cousins." Mrs. Dirning lets us come in a few minutes after the nine o'clock curfew when we go to the movies. And next week is the freshmen initiation party in the gym. I hear we all have to dress up weird, like in baby clothes or something, and the seniors blindfold us and feed us peeled grapes and tell us they're eyeballs—stuff like that. It'll be fun."

Anna wrinkled her nose. Kids' idea of fun...? She smiled at her daughter—what a different attitude from the Monday morning journey.

"So, do you like your classes and your teachers?"

"Yeah, it's really different from grade school. We have to go to a new room for each class. I really like my English teacher. We're going to read *Hamlet* and then act it out—I think it's going to be fun. And I'm taking typing, and home ec, and PE."

Monica stopped her recitation for a moment. "The only class I really don't like is algebra. I just don't get it. Mr. Burns doesn't really explain it, he just gives us the answers to the next day's assignment and tells us to work out the problems until we get that answer. Well, then we exchange papers to correct, and of course, everybody has the right answer and nobody marks off for not working the problem. I brought my book home, Dad, do you think you could help me understand it?"

Anna smiled, full of happy pride. How sweet. Asking Dad for help.

Neil turned a big smile toward his daughter. "Sure, honey, I'd be happy to." He reached over to pat Anna's hand as though to say, "See, I told you she'd be all right."

CHAPTER FIVE

The mood in the auditorium was hushed, as Anna and Neil sat with dozens of other parents in the semi-darkness, nervously waiting for the spring recital to begin. Anna squirmed in her seat, twisted her hanky, took a small compact from her purse and checked her teeth for lipstick smears.

Monica had been practicing Beethoven's *Moonlight Sonata* for months, in anticipation of this regional high school music festival competition in Miles City. Every day she played for hours, memorizing every note, every *pianissimo*, every *legato*, every *crescendo*. Anna had heard it so many times she thought she could almost play the piece herself.

She hoped Monica wouldn't get so nervous that she would lose her place. Anna's own stomach crawled, but her heart overflowed with pride. She reached for Neil's hand as Monica's name was announced. He squeezed back.

She leaned forward as Monica came on stage. After the first few bars, the tension in Anna's shoulders eased, and she leaned back in her seat, enjoying the familiar music. Neil let out his breath and relaxed beside her. The last chord died away, and Monica stood up to bow. For a moment there was nothing but silence, and time seemed to stop. A little ping of fear stabbed through Anna; then the swell of applause lifted and carried her as though she had been up there on the stage. She and Neil stared at each other with wet eyes and wide, Cheshire-cat grins, both wildly clapping until their hands ached. The eight years of piano lessons had paid off.

Monica was all smiles. "I did my best, Mom. At least I didn't lose my place, and I didn't make too many mistakes. But man, that makes me so nervous. I don't know why I do it."

35

"Because you're so good at it." Neil smiled at his daughter. "And you got a number one rating. I'm so proud of you."

"What did you think of the band? Pretty pathetic, huh?" Monica laughed. The Foster High School band had received the lowest possible rating.

"There are a lot of new kids in band this year. They'll do better next year, especially with you in the trombone section," her dad said. "I remember playing the trumpet in band at the festival and being scared to death I was going to make a mistake. Your chorus sounded good, though."

Monica wrinkled her nose. "Yeah, but we only got a number two rating."

"Second is wonderful, honey." Anna patted her daughter's shoulder.

They stopped in Foster at the Stockman's Cafe for coffee and pie. Several other parents were there with their kids.

"Congratulations on your piano solo," someone called out.

"Yeah, you sounded just like Van Cliburn," added another boy from the band.

"You must be very proud," said one of the mothers, stopping by their table. "Those kids sure work hard, and they do very well for being from a small town like Foster."

Anna beamed, her cheeks flushed with happiness. She was so proud of Monica she thought she'd burst. For so long, she'd been made fun of, but since she was in high school, wherever they went, people remarked about her—even included Kevin and Lizzie—how polite and nice-looking and smart they were, how well they did in school.

"We have fine kids, don't we?" She smiled at Neil.

"Yes, we do. And I have a fine wife."

That evening, after the kids had gone to bed, Anna and Neil sat sipping a glass of wine and looked through a scrapbook dedicated to their children's achievements.

Anna pasted the program from the piano competition on a page. "I'm so proud of Monica's performance today. She has certainly overcome her shyness, to be able to get up on that stage in front of everybody."

Neil nodded. "She was great. I don't think I could've done that."

She turned back a few pages. "I'm proud of Kevin, too, and even Lizzie." After a rocky start with a bad teacher in first grade, Kevin, in fifth grade, enjoyed school more now, and was making good grades. He liked to read, but with less obsession than Monica. He'd rather be outside, building a go-cart, or taking something apart so he could put it back together.

When he was eight, he had built a guitar from an old hubcap and a lid from a plastic gallon container. She smiled. He had carved the neck out of a two-by-four board and bent wire over it to make the finished product. It actually sounded somewhat like a real guitar. He wasn't interested in piano lessons, even though Monica had tried to teach him, but he did strum a guitar now and then.

"Remember this?" She pointed to a picture of Kevin and his dog on a raft. In spring, when he was about seven, the creeks had overflowed and flooded the hay bottom near the house. Kevin built a raft from old boards, and Anna'd been shocked one afternoon to see him poling his way across the small shallow lake. Her heart in her throat, she ran out to rescue him if he fell in.

She paged back to his baby pictures. Kevin had begun his life so very small and thin. He was a finicky eater, and she had taken him to the doctor several times, worried that he was undernourished. Then, he'd developed severe allergies and asthma and had nearly died once after an outing to a park in town. In the summer, he couldn't even go near a hayfield without his eyes swelling shut.

But he was still "all boy," always outside, tinkering alongside his dad, "working on engines," fixing the tractor or changing the oil in the truck. Neil looked at a picture of Kevin at age five, holding a wrench nearly as big as he. "Yup, he takes after his old man."

"He's so emotionally sensitive, though." Anna sighed. Kevin was very much in tune with social injustice, always siding with the "underdog," unable to understand how people could be so cruel.

"How is he going to make his way in the world away from home?" He was her only son, and she felt an overwhelming need to shield him from an insensitive world. He needed her protection. She simply couldn't let anything happen to him.

Neil caressed her hand. "He'll do just fine, *Liebchen*. You'll just have to let him go when the time comes."

Anna blinked back a tear and turned a few more pages. "Then there's Lizzie."

The second-grader was bright, maybe smarter than the other two, Anna suspected, but she refused to apply herself to anything. Projects were never finished, books never read, homework forgotten. She was constantly on the move, always defiant. If Anna said the sky was blue, Lizzie would argue with her. She was forever getting into fights at school and having to stay inside during recess, having broken some rule again.

Neil nodded. "She certainly is an enigma."

Anna shook her head. "I don't know how to deal with her sometimes. She frustrates me to no end."

"Maybe I need to take her out to work with me more. Tire her out." Neil grinned.

"Maybe so." Anna flipped through more photo pages. Nevertheless, she was proud of her youngest. Lizzie had the most exquisite singing voice at such a young age, and she sang often. Anna would stop still, just drinking in the clear, high notes— almost angelic, she thought. Ironic. If she could just keep her singing all the time....

~~~

One January afternoon the following winter, Anna sat down to knit, taking a rare time of rest. The kids were in their rooms, and Neil was reading a book. At the sound of a pickup approaching, she jumped up from the sofa. "Oh, no. Company.

I thought we were going to have a nice, quiet Sunday afternoon. Oh, it's the Gharretts. And I don't have anything baked." She sighed. "I wish they'd called first."

Evelyn breezed in, after removing her snow boots inside the enclosed entry. "Hi, everybody. We thought you might like some company. Since we invited ourselves, I brought some date bars." She handed a covered plate to Anna, her hazel eyes laughing. "Lana brought her ice skates. Do Kevin and Lizzie want to go skating?"

"Yeah," squealed Lizzie. "C'mon, Lana. I'll beat you in a race this time. Mom, where are my skates?" Even though Lana was thirteen and Lizzie only eight, Anna's youngest never recognized the age difference as an obstacle.

"Here, I'll help you find them." Kevin called out from his bedroom. "I think they're in here somewhere."

Neil bundled up, joined Evelyn's husband, Bud, and tossed shovels into the back of the pickup. The kids skated on the reservoirs where the cows watered, and the men would often have to shovel snow off the surface first. It had become a common Sunday afternoon outing for the neighbors to get together around the frozen ponds to watch their kids skate. Sometimes they built a bonfire, roasted hotdogs and made hot chocolate with marshmallows.

Monica shot out of her room, where she had been studying. "Did I hear someone mention skating?"

Evelyn smiled. "Well, I thought the younger ones could entertain themselves. I brought a new piece of music. I'm supposed to sing at the VFW Ladies' Auxiliary luncheon next week, and I thought maybe you and I could work on it."

"Oh." Monica's eager expression collapsed. "Sure." She went to the piano. "Let me play through it a little, try it out first."

While Anna made coffee and the rest of the group went off to skate, Monica and Evelyn practiced "Born Free" from the new movie. Then they went on to some old-time favorites just for fun—"Mairsy Doats and Dozy Doats," "Buttons and Bows," and "My Wild Irish Rose."

Anna hummed along as she bustled around the kitchen. She loved to listen to Monica's playing and enjoyed Evelyn's singing. She thought her daughter was beginning to relax a little and maybe have fun with it. It was good for her—she was too serious.

Evelyn was a nice woman, warm and friendly. Anna believed she could get to like her. She pictured them exchanging confidences over a cup of coffee and laughing over their children's latest escapades. Anna shook her head and frowned. She'd gotten friendly with Vickie Thompson, and she had just up and moved away. And whenever Anna had confided in any of the other neighbor women, it had almost immediately come back to her on the gossip chain, all twisted grotesquely out of context. Maybe it was better not to. But… she needed a friend. Could she trust someone after all?

The coffee was ready, and Anna, still humming, set out the good china cups and dessert plates for the ritual that she loved so much. In Germany it had been a social time, a time of sharing and laughter, and she was glad the tradition was the same in America. Before they'd gotten telephones, everyone had gone visiting on Sunday afternoons. It was the social event of the week in the Horse Creek neighborhood. But now, since they were all on the party line, listening in on each other's conversations had taken the place of the Sunday coffee klatch. So, even though she grumbled about drop-in company, in her heart Anna was glad that Evelyn had come.

Her thoughts were interrupted as the outside door crashed open. Kevin yelled, "Mom! Mom! Come quick!"

Monica stopped playing in mid-chord, and the three women rushed out into the enclosed porch.

"What's wrong?" Anna looked at her son's ashen face.

"Dad fell on the ice. I think he broke his leg. Bud says we need to get him to the hospital right away. Hurry."

Anna gasped. "Oh no, what happened?"

"He just stepped onto the edge of the reservoir, and his legs went out from under him," Bud explained. "He landed with the weight on top of his right leg on a ridge of ice. I heard it snap." He grimaced, his sun-dried face wrinkling in sympathy.

Anna turned to Evelyn and Monica. "The kids..."

Evelyn put a hand on her arm. "It's okay. We'll take care of them, get them fed."

Anna gave Neil aspirin for the pain and held his hand, talking to him soothingly as Bud sped over the thirty-five-mile-long road to Foster.

At the hospital Doc Farnum gave Neil a shot for pain and set his leg. "Now you'll just have to take it easy for a few weeks." Doc smeared the last of the plaster on Neil's cast. "But you'll be mended and back to work in no time."

Anna gulped. It was winter, and the feeding had to be done every day. How would they manage? Maybe Kevin could help her in the mornings and go to school late. At eleven, he'd already proved to be a great help.

She smiled at Neil. "Okay, honey. Let's go home."

"Oh boy," he fretted on the way home. "How am I going to keep the cows fed? Take care of things?"

"Don't worry." Bud glanced over his shoulder at them. "I'll come by and help."

~~~

The skies turned blustery, and over the next few days the ominous clouds spit snow off and on, like grumpy old men, restless and ornery. Bud Gharrett came every other day to help Anna feed. She was grateful that Kevin didn't have to miss school, and for the time being, the cows could get by on this feeding schedule.

About a week after Neil's accident, Anna awoke to him gasping for breath next to her.

"Wake up, honey, what's wrong?"

He moaned, tossing his head back and forth on the pillow. She felt his forehead. He was burning with fever. *Ach du lieber*, now what? She slid out of bed onto the icy floor, groping for her robe and slippers. Slipping an aspirin tablet between his lips, she made him drink a glass of water. Then she spent the remainder of the night holding cold, wet cloths to his forehead. Did he have pneumonia? Surely it wasn't the mono again. She'd thought back then she might lose him. The fears hovered over her like demons in the night.

As soon as it was light, Anna called Bud Gharrett.

"Sounds like we'd better get him into the hospital," he volunteered.

She got the kids ready for school, Lizzie fighting her every step of the way. Anna's patience had worn thin an as old dishtowel. "All right, Miss Elizabeth Annette Moser, you straighten up right NOW!" Finally, they were ready, and she and Bud dropped them at the schoolhouse on their way to Foster.

At the hospital, Doc Farnum agreed with Anna's diagnosis. "Looks like he's developed pneumonia. I'm going to get him on penicillin and admit him for a few days, so I can keep an eye on him."

The wind had picked up by the time Anna and Bud headed for home, and by evening the clouds were no longer merely threatening, but had begun to vent their anger with a vengeance. The January blizzard had begun.

"Is Dad going to be okay?" Kevin asked as soon as he got in the car outside the school.

"They're taking very good care of him in the hospital, honey." Anna tried to make her voice sound reassuring, as much for her own benefit as for his.

The house was chilly, so she fired up the oil stove in the living room, and warmed up a hot stew for supper.

"Mommy, it's freezing cold in here," Lizzie whined as Anna got the kids ready for bed. She scratched an opening in the frost on the window and looked out at the thermometer. "Thirty-five below zero. No wonder you're cold." She left the tap running a trickle in the kitchen sink to keep the water line from freezing, piled extra blankets on their beds, and crawled into her own, still wearing her long wool underwear and an extra sweater.

At eleven o'clock, Anna woke up shivering, despite her warm clothes. Lizzie whimpered in the next room. The wind shrieked like a wild, wounded creature. She got up and scratched a hole in the window frost. The thermometer read minus fifty. In the living room, she put her hand on the oil burner. Cold. The fire had gone out, the oil too thick to run.

"*Himmel.*" Anna flicked the light switch, thinking she could go turn on the electric oven in the kitchen for heat. Nothing. The electricity was out, too.

Anna dressed Kevin and Lizzie in woolen socks and put knitted hats on their heads, their breath forming frosty puffs in the air. "Come, kids, get into bed with me." She grabbed their extra blankets and piled them on top of her bed. Even the dog, Fritzi, joined them.

It was the coldest night Anna could ever remember. She'd certainly never experienced anything like this in Germany. Images of the cows frozen stiff in the pasture chased through her mind, and she hoped they'd had enough sense to find shelter in the coulees.

A sudden thought gave her an internal chill. Surely the hospital had back-up generators so it wouldn't be without heat too. And the dorm. *Ach du lieber Gott, please take care of my Neil and Monica.*

The three of them huddled together to wait out the long, bleak hours until morning.

CHAPTER SIX

Teeth chattering, Anna slipped out of bed in the gray early morning light. She shivered uncontrollably as she picked up the phone to call the Stokleys at the store. No dial tone. Oh no, the phone lines were down, too.

She crawled back into bed, arms around Kevin and Lizzie, and prayed for the electricity to come back on, so she could at least fix something hot to eat and turn on the oven to warm the kitchen. Anna grimaced a wry smile. She'd never thought she would miss that dirty old coal stove. But sometimes these modern conveniences weren't so convenient.

"I'm cold and hungry, Mom," Lizzie whimpered.

Nearly-frozen pieces of bread didn't do much to alleviate their hunger. It was almost noon, and Anna wondered for the umpteenth time how she could cook something hot for them, when she heard an engine outside. She slipped from under the pile of covers and pulled on her boots and overcoat. Bud Gharrett and Bill Mitchell were at the door.

"Are you all right?" Bud stomped his feet and pounded the feeling back into his arms. "Dang, it's nippy out there."

Anna laughed, a hysterical note of relief in her voice. "We're okay. A little cold, though. The fuel line seems to be frozen up, and the oil stove went out."

"We'll thaw it out for you in a minute. Just want to get in out of that wind a bit," Mitchell said. "With the wind chill, it's gotta be seventy-five below."

Anna rubbed her cold hands. "Come, sit. I'm sorry, I can't even offer you something hot to help you warm up. Do you know when the electricity will be back on?"

Mitchell shook his head. "Hard to say. But I brought a generator. We'll get that hooked up for you, and you'll be able to cook soon."

The men did that first, so Anna could turn on the kitchen stove. Then they set up a makeshift shelter outside with sheets of plywood around the fuel tank, and with a blowtorch, thawed the fuel line that fed into the house.

They came in to light the oil stove. "We re-wrapped the line and you may want to leave that shelter up. Hope that'll keep it from freezing again." Bud shivered. "I think the wind is dyin' down a little." Now that the coffee was brewed, he gratefully accepted it, wrapped his colorless fingers around the hot cup and held it close to his face, inhaling the steam.

Mitchell took a sip of his coffee. "That was smart of you to leave the water runnin' so that line didn't freeze."

"Thank you both so much. I don't know what I would've done if we'd had another night like that." Anna could hardly believe the goodness of her neighbors. Just for her—did that mean she was finally being accepted? She blinked. "You really risked yourselves, coming out in this blizzard."

"Nah. It ain't that bad out." Bud sipped the coffee. "Heck, I remember ridin' herd one winter during a blizzard so bad that when my horse froze to death, I had to cut 'im open and crawl inside to keep from freezin' m'self."

The kids stared at him, wide-eyed. "Wow. You really did that?" Lizzie asked.

"Yup. Hated to lose that ol' horse, but he sure saved my life that day." Bud grinned and winked at Anna.

The next day the blizzard finally ceased its angry tirade, blowing a few last feeble gusts, then gave up with a sigh as the sun crested the white bluffs. From its great distance in the winter sky, Old Sol tried to melt the ice crystals floating in the air, but offered only brilliance instead of warmth.

Anna opened the porch door, pushing a mound of snow ahead of it. She looked around in astonishment from the lee-side of the house. On the north and west sides, snowdrifts caressed the bottom of the window sills. Out in the yard, the vehicles were just memories under mounds of white.

"How am I going to get the cows fed?" Then a pang of fear hit. "I sure hope we haven't lost any."

Anna and Kevin shoveled a path to the barn to check on the milk cow, the horses and chickens. "Oh no." Anna saw that several chickens had been smothered when the flock bunched together for warmth, but was relieved to see the other animals were alive—cold and hungry probably, but okay. Kevin climbed to the top of the haystack behind the log structure, dug out a couple of bales and threw them down. He squinted up the slope toward the county road. "Hey, Mom, somebody's plowing out our road!"

Anna clawed her way to the top of the snow-covered stack. Sure enough, here came a big tractor with a blade, furrowing a path through the drifts. It was Bud Gharrett, back again. He waved as he pulled up into the hay yard.

"You guys still alive?" He hopped down from the huge machine, carrying a couple of grocery sacks. "Brought ya some grub and your mail. Thought maybe I'd plow a road out to the pasture and see if we can get your cows fed."

"Oh, that would be wonderful!" Anna cried. "Thank you. You're a real life saver."

"God bless you," she whispered as he drove off.

~~~

Anna greeted Monica with a bear hug after her daughter had caught a ride home after school on Friday. With a great surge of relief at having her home, Anna bustled around fixing her dinner, fussing over her.

Monica draped her arms around Kevin and Lizzy while Anna told her about the blizzard. "Boy, I had no idea you guys were so cold out here. We were chilly in the dorm, but the coal furnace kept on working, and we never lost electricity. I went to visit Dad after the blizzard, and everyone was fine at the hospital, too."

That weekend, Monica and Kevin helped Anna feed the cows and chop the ice out of the water tanks in the pasture, while Lizzie played in the snow with the collie, Fritzi—almost normal activities. Anna felt practically giddy at having come through the blizzard and now sharing time with her kids.

"Thank God for those deep coulees out here in this pasture. The herd was sheltered during the storm, and we only lost that one old cow," Anna said. "And I'm doubly thankful for our neighbors. I don't know what I would've done…" She tossed hay bales down from the stack to where Monica and Kevin arranged them in the back of the pickup.

Monica smiled. "Yeah, you guys were lucky."

In another week, they went to Foster to bring a pale, weak Neil home. Doc Farnum took her aside and whispered, "A blood clot traveled from the broken leg up through Neil's lung. You're lucky he's still around."

Anna gasped and shuddered as a cold chill passed through her. How close she'd been to losing him yet again. She had no idea what she would have done if he had died.

~~~

Neil recovered slowly through the winter, with Bud and other neighbors coming by to help feed. Finally, Chinook winds brought the promise of spring, with more than the usual flooding and mud everywhere. It was difficult to find a piece of dry ground in the pasture to spread out hay for the cattle, and Neil and Anna watched every day for the first signs of green.

One Friday, when they picked up Monica at school, she started to cry as soon as she got into the car. "What's wrong, honey?" Anna turned toward the back seat and peered into her daughter's face.

"I got in trouble at school today." She sobbed.

Anna's heart skipped a beat. Trouble. *Ach, Himmel. Curfew? Boys?* "What kind of trouble?"

"The school paper." Monica gulped. "They didn't like... a story... I wrote."

Neil turned and gave her a quick glance. "What do you mean, they didn't like it?"

This simply brought more sobs. Anna reached over the seat and patted her shoulder.

Monica had volunteered to work on the school newspaper, *The Sagebrush Saga,* and she loved it. Here was an area where she could hone her writing skills.

"Come on, honey, tell us about it." Gradually, Anna pried the story from her.

"Mom, so many times I'm the only one who works on the paper after school. I have to type and retype to justify columns on mimeograph paper and then run off copies."

Monica often wrote many of the articles, typed them up and did the layout all on her own. Anna was so proud of her efforts—her daughter doing something she'f never even dreamed of attempting. The journalism advisor was lavish with his praise to Neil and Anna.

Anna frowned. "But Mr. Cadbury says you work so hard and do such a good job."

"Last night I worked late to finish the edition so it could be run off and distributed today. It was almost curfew and I realized I still had a hole on the front page that needed to be filled." Monica rummaged in her book bag. "I thought of the campaign to build a new grade school in Foster, so I wrote an editorial." She handed Anna a copy of what she'd written and Anna read it aloud.

...Education is not defined by the building. Some of the best teaching was done in dugouts by the pioneers... Perhaps the money would be of better use to hire more teachers. What does it matter

that students have a fancy new building if the quality of education is lacking...?

Neil nodded. "Hmm. Very insightful."

Anna smiled. Her girl was so mature, venturing her opinion on such an issue. Not something she would be brave enough to do. She always tried to avoid controversy. Her stomach cramped. Controversy caused too much pain and disappointment.

Monica hmphed. "Then I'm sitting in study hall this morning, when Mr. Cadbury comes in and takes me to the principal's office."

Anna raised her eyebrows.

"Principal Felix slapped a copy of the paper on the counter in front of me and asked if I'd written the editorial." Monica bit her trembling lower lip. "Then he asked me who put me up to it. I told him nobody. That I...I was working late last night and just, just needed a filler. He kept asking, 'Did you really just write that last night?' and he accused you guys of putting me up to this."

Anna blinked. Good grief. Here was the principal thinking she and Neil did everything for Monica, too, just like those 4-H women. She shook her head. "Oh, honey."

"Then he said I hadn't let him or Mr. Cadbury read it first, 'cause they have to approve the paper." Her eyes shone bright with tears. "But I did. I left the original pages on Mr. Felix's desk last night. And when I didn't see any corrections this morning, I went ahead and ran them off."

"Sounds logical." Neil glanced at her in the rear-view mirror.

"Well, Mr. Felix said he didn't see them. He said it was unacceptable, and he told Mr. Cadbury to go into everyone's locker and retrieve the newspaper. It wouldn't be distributed." Monica hiccupped. "I didn't know I'd done anything wrong. All I did was write my opinion. That's what an editorial is, isn't it?"

Neil's face turned stormy. "Darn right it is."

"Mr. Cadbury was angry, too. He didn't even stick up for me. He said it's a controversial subject in the community, and it doesn't look good if our paper comes out with an editorial against the new school." Monica doubled over in the back seat of the car, held her stomach and tried to bite back her sobs. "I didn't know."

Anna looked at Neil, helpless. What an awful situation. She should have protected her daughter from something like this. She reached over the seat and smoothed her daughter's hair. "I'm so sorry, honey. There, there, it's okay." She tried to make her voice soothing, as though she were rocking a baby to sleep.

Through her own pain, a wave of pride welled up inside her. That took guts. But, what would people think? A nervous twitch began just below her right eye.

She could hear the gossip already—"Funny ideas those Germans have. They're teaching their kids to be subversives." It always came back to being a German. If word got out that their daughter had written such an inflammatory article, it could be embarrassing for them all, maybe hurtful for Monica. People would make fun of her, like they'd made fun of Anna.

As they walked into the house, the phone was ringing. Neil picked it up and Anna could hear Monica's former grade school teacher, Dallas. Her voice boomed from the receiver. "...heard what happened at the high school... outright censorship... unconstitutional, not to mention unconscionable. What are these so-called educators teaching these days, anyway? It's horse-puckey! I'd like your permission to send that article in to the *Foster Tribune*. Everyone needs to know about this censorship."

Neil hesitated and glanced at Anna. "Well, we just found out about it ourselves. Let's hold off on any action right now. We need to think it over. But thanks for your support." He replaced the receiver slowly, furrows splitting his brow.

"That's very noble of Dallas." Anna sighed. "But no, I don't think we want to make waves in the community. Let's just let it die a natural death."

Monica sat, wide-eyed and stunned. Then she got up and went to her room, mumbling, "Every time I express my thoughts, I get in trouble."

Anna's heart wrenched. *Is she turning into a version of me?* So many times she had been stung that very same way, until she'd become too afraid to say anything for fear it would come back like a boomerang with a sharp barb.

~~~

Neil slumped heavily onto the couch, his stomach churning for his daughter. He balled up his fists. His first instinct was to fight this. What on earth were people thinking? They couldn't get away with censorship on a high school newspaper. He looked at Anna. The telltale redness of embarrassment and anger stained her neck and her eyes glistened with tears.

"I think we should let Dallas run the story in the town paper," he said.

Anna's sharp intake of breath pierced his ire. She shook her head. "Why start a fight? We're not that kind. We don't cause trouble with our neighbors."

Neil sighed. He was so tired; he didn't yet have a lot of stamina since his bout with pneumonia and the blood clot. Besides, ranch people didn't go looking for trouble. They needed each other to help out, even to survive at times. He didn't want to create enemies either.

"You know I agree with that. Prejudice and controversy will find us wherever we are, it seems. Like the Bible says, 'Sufficient is the trouble of the day...'" He turned to his beloved wife and drew in a breath. "*Liebchen...* you've been here for almost twenty years. Why does what the neighbors think still bother you so much?"

Anna's eyes filled with tears. "What people thought almost caused me not to be able to come to America, to you. What people thought of me, a German, and my accent caused me so much embarrassment, so much loneliness when I first arrived. I was always an outsider. I wanted to hide sometimes. I didn't want anyone to notice me." Her voice choked. "I still feel that way sometimes."

She stood. "That principal!" Her voice rose and she paced the room. "He hurt my daughter and embarrassed her. I can't let that happen. I'd like to..." She clenched her fists. "I'd like to go in to that high school and rip that man's head off!"

She gasped and sank into the sofa next to Neil. "What am I doing? What am I saying?" Her lip quivered. "I don't want Monica to have to go through that much pain. I only want to protect her." She burst into helpless sobs.

Neil turned and wrapped his arms around her. He felt her pain flow into his heart and he rocked her while her tears wet the front of his shirt. Tears trickled down his cheeks too.

They sat entwined for a long time until both were spent.

He looked up to see Monica standing in the doorway of her bedroom, anguish twisting her face. When their eyes met, she turned and shut the door.

~~~

Neil glanced over at Monica, hunched stony-faced in the passenger seat, as he drove her back to school on Monday. What could he say to make her feel better? He felt like he was caught between two of those big sandstone boulders out in the pasture. Trouble is, he could understand both his wife and his daughter, but he couldn't think of anything to do to ease the pain for either. This wasn't like fixing a tractor.

He cleared his throat. "I'm sorry about the newspaper incident, honey. You know your mom and I are very proud of you, don't you?"

She snorted and turned to stare out the window.

Oh Lord, give me the wisdom I need right now. Neil accelerated over the last hill into Foster. "Your mom... She has never really felt accepted here. The war was hard on her, but people still hold being a German against her."

Monica turned to look at him. "I know it's been hard for her, and people haven't treated her nice, but why do we still have to be so secretive all the time? I don't even know what I can do or say anymore, because I'm afraid I'll get into trouble."

Neil sighed. "Good question." On he didn't know the answer to. He pulled the car up in front of the school. "Say, why don't we go in and talk to Mr. Felix right now."

His daughter's eyes filled with tears. "You would?"

He opened the car door. "Yes, let's."

In the high school office, the principal rose from behind his desk and stuck out his hand for Neil to shake. "Good morning, Mr. Moser. What can I do for you today?"

Neil took a fortifying breath. "I want to talk to you about the censorship of Monica's editorial last Friday. That doesn't seem like a good way to teach journalism."

Felix ducked his head. "Yeah. Well, it was an unfortunate incident, but this is a controversial subject, and the high school is governed by the same board as the elementary school, so…" He spread his hands, palms up.

Neil glanced at the door to see Mr. Cadbury standing in the opening. He swept a look from one to the other. "So you're not backing your student in expressing her free speech opinion."

"I'm sorry. The decision stands. There's nothing I can do." Felix sat behind his desk and pulled a stack of files toward him.

Monica stood like a statue, her face pale.

Anger simmered like a stewpot inside Neil. Before he lost it entirely and did something he'd regret, he gestured to Monica, and they stepped out into the hallway.

Tears filled her blue eyes. "See what I mean?" She shrugged. "Might as well get my suitcase out of the car and take it to the dorm."

Neil opened the double door, and they stepped outside. As they turned toward the car, he heard a voice.

"Mr. Moser, Monica." Mr. Cadbury stepped out behind them. "I apologize to you both. I know this was upsetting to you, Monica, but my hands are tied. My job here is on the line." He gave them a weak smile. "You are my best student. That article took courage to write, and I want you to know I am proud of you."

As Monica stood rooted to the spot, her mouth agape, the teacher turned and went back into the building. She turned to Neil, her face red and contorted. "He's 'proud' of me, but he can't support me." She huffed out a breath. "Well, that is that."

"It seems like things are pretty much set in stone." He sighed, strode to the car to get her suitcase, and gave his daughter a hug. "Stay strong, honey. Don't let this discourage you."

She gave a forced smile. "Sure, Dad. See ya on Friday."

CHAPTER SEVEN

Evelyn stuck her head in the kitchen door. "We're going to Foster. Do you need anything from town?"

Anna turned from the sink and shook the soapsuds from her hands. "Hi there. You're on your way early today." She picked up a towel. "Yes, I could use a twenty-five-pound bag of flour, if you're sure it's no trouble."

"Not at all," came the cheerful reply. "We'll be back this afternoon. See ya then."

Anna finished the dishes, then gathered up a load of clothes to throw into her new electric, avocado-colored washer, with matching dryer. She hummed to herself as she selected the water level and temperature and poured a cup of detergent into the drum. She could hardly believe the luxury. Just a few months ago, Neil had finished building an addition to the house, enlarging the living room, adding bedrooms for the girls and an indoor bathroom. Although Anna loved the bathroom—no more brushing snow off the outhouse seat in the winter—she liked her washer and dryer even better. No more frozen clothes on the clothesline in winter.

While the washing machine churned, Anna remembered how she once had to wash clothes. For the first couple of years after they had moved to the Horse Creek ranch, she had done laundry on a washboard by hand. Then Neil picked up a washing machine with a Briggs and Stratton motor, and Anna had thought she was in heaven—well, almost. Before they installed running water to the kitchen sink, she'd had to fetch water in from the well, heat it on the stove, and then carry buckets of the hot water to fill the machine.

Later, even with hot running water installed, she still had to carry it. So, she had done all of the washing in one tubful of water. First the whites, feeding each piece from the washer through a hand-turned wringer into a tub of cold water for rinsing by hand. And then everything had to go through the wringer again. Next came the light colors, followed by gradually darker colors, then the denim overalls. Last came the dirty throw rugs. By the time she was ready to carry the water out again, it had turned to a light shade of mud.

Now finally, in 1967, her house was all modern, and she could do one load of wash or several, as she wanted, instead of spending a long, hard day once a week, getting it all done. And yes, the bathroom was a real luxury, too. Now Monica would be able to bring her friends home from school on weekends. No more embarrassing outdoor toilet. Anna remembered the first night Monica had slept in her new room. She had arrived home late, after a track meet, and instead of having the foldout couch made up in the living room, Anna and Neil had blindfolded her. Each took an arm and led her into the room. They'd painted it a pale green, and white sheer curtains with yellow daisies fluttered at the window.

"Oh wow. Mom, Dad. Far out! I can't believe it. It's finally done." Monica pranced around, digging her toes into the gold carpet. "Oh, I don't know if I'll be able to sleep tonight. This is so groovy."

Anna folded the clean clothes and started for her bedroom. Her pleasant reverie was shattered by the shrill ringing of the phone. They'd had a phone for seven years now, but it still startled her when it rang, and she still disliked talking on it.

"Hello?" She heard only sobs. "Hello, who is this? I can't understand you."

"... Evelyn... car... wreck... hospital," was all she could understand between gulps and sobs.

"Evelyn? You were in an accident? Are you all right?"

"No... Bud ... He's dead!" The last came out as a wail.

A chill washed over Anna and she collapsed into a chair. "Oh, my word, Evelyn." Her hand shook as she pressed the receiver to her ear. "We'll come right in. Hang on, we'll be there soon."

A nurse came on the phone then to tell Anna that Evelyn's leg was broken and she would need help as soon as she was released.

"Neil! Neil!" Anna ran across the yard to the shop.

He stuck his head out the door, a worried look already on his face. "What's wrong?"

"It's the Gharretts. They've been in an accident, and Bud's been killed."

"Oh dear God, we'd better stop by and pick up Lana from school."

Anna bit her lip. How would they tell the girl her dad had been killed?

~~~

Anna propped a pillow on the kitchen chair under Evelyn's cast and turned to get the coffeepot and a plate of cookies. Two weeks since the accident, and Evelyn and Lana had been staying with the Mosers after Evelyn was released from the hospital. Her eyes were continually red from crying.

"What am I going to do without Bud?" She couldn't seem to think beyond the fact she was now alone, with no one to care for her. "I don't know what to do."

Anna poured the coffee. She was at a loss for words of further comfort. They'd been over this. Again and again. "Can you go stay with relatives? Will the Wickers let you stay on the place for a while and take care of some of the chores until they hire someone else?" She set her cup down, sloshing coffee into the saucer. "Maybe the Stokleys would hire you at the store." But nothing seemed to appeal to Evelyn.

Anna tried to be understanding; after all, how would *she* feel if she lost Neil? She raised her eyes upward. Heaven forbid. "Well, you just stay here until you get that cast off; then you can think about what you're going to do." Her heart softened. She owed Evelyn. Bud had been so good to them last winter when Neil was in the hospital.

She glanced at her and Neil's closed bedroom door. Monica holed up in there to study since Evelyn and Lana were staying in her room, and Monica was back to sleeping on the couch on weekends. With their long-term guests, Anna hardly had a chance to talk to her daughter. But she knew something was bothering her. She sighed. She also knew Evelyn's need for a friend was most urgent. Anna had to help. Did she dare open her heart, and possibly be hurt again?

Monica was a junior in high school and was strong and self-sufficient. She could get by without her mother's extra attention awhile longer.

By the time Evelyn's leg healed, six months of normal family life had been disrupted, and Monica wasn't speaking to either of them. Neil and Kevin spent all their spare time outside, and of course, Lizzie wouldn't cooperate in any way to help.

Finally, Evelyn announced she had a job cooking at the huge ranch about fifteen miles west of Horse Creek on the way to Wynona.

Anna patted the other woman's shoulder. "That's wonderful." At the same time, she mentally kicked up her heels and shouted, *Hooray, I have my family back!* Now, maybe she could take that extra time with Monica and see if their rift could be healed.

~~~

Atop the growing haystack, Anna swept the straw hat off her head, fanned her face, and wiped the sweat from her brow with the oversized red kerchief she wore around her neck. She should talk to her daughter. She took a deep breath. *Now's as good a time as any.*

"Well... how are things going at school?"

Monica looked at her sharply and shrugged. "Fine."

"Any more problems with the school paper?"

"No. It's fine."

Anna sighed. "I feel like I kind of let you down when that all happened, and then Evelyn and Lana were here for so long, and we never got to talk about it."

Her daughter was silent for a moment. "It's okay. There was nothing anybody could do about it. It's over and done."

Anna nodded and fanned her face again. *Just like her dad—he doesn't want to talk about things either.*

Monica reached down and tried to flutter the air with the heavy leather chaps she wore over her jeans to keep the sharp ends of the cut hay from scratching her legs. She looked up at the relentless ball of fire in the clear blue sky. "Man, it's hot. Aren't we going to take a break pretty soon?"

"Yeah, where's a cloud when you need it?" Anna looked across the field to where Neil approached with another load of bales to be stacked, like bricks, just so—one layer headed crossways, then next lengthwise, tying in the rows underneath, so the stack wouldn't fall down. Anna and Monica stumbled to the opposite end of the stack while Neil dumped the load where they'd been working. She waved to get his attention and mimed drinking a cup of coffee. He nodded and backed the stacker away while they took care of the bales.

She stuck her sharp hay hook into one end with a flick of the wrist, while Monica did the same on the other end. Together, they hauled the fifty-pound bale to just the right spot on the stack, and repeated the process until all were in place. Then Neil slid the fork onto the stack and gave them an elevator ride to the ground.

He grabbed an insulated cooler from the pickup. Bone-weary and sticky with sweat, they all headed for the shady side of the stack, where a slight breeze was blowing. The women stripped off their boots and extra layers of heavy protective clothing, fanning themselves.

"It's a miserable hot day." Anna poured coffee and lemonade and dug out canned peaches and chocolate chip cookies from the cooler.

"It's not so bad out on the stacker. Driving creates a breeze." Neil chuckled. "Too bad you don't know how to drive this backwards machine." Neil had built what was called a "farmhand" on the chassis of an old truck.

Monica rolled her eyes and leaned back against the haystack.

Anna knew she hated this job more than any other on the ranch. "Slave labor," Monica had mumbled more than once. She didn't seem to mind baling the hay—she could wear her cut-offs and halter top and get a tan while driving around on the tractor. Monica was probably envious of the town girls who didn't have to do this kind of work. They just hung around all summer, getting a tan, doing their nails and taking an occasional stroll to the Tastee Freeze to check out the guys driving around. Talk about lazy. She didn't want her daughter to "lay around" sunning herself and not learn to work. Too bad Kevin had such terrible asthma and couldn't help with the haying. But then, somebody had to keep an eye on Lizzie. Anna took a bite of cookie.

"Saw Ed Roberts at the store this morning." Neil's voice interrupted her thoughts. "Said he'd heard that the Wynona Bank was being investigated for some shady land deals."

"Hmmm." Anna sipped her coffee. "Did his brother George ever get his ranch back?"

"Nope. Ed said he and a bunch of others who had their places foreclosed by Morgan filed a complaint with the banking commission." He held out his cup for more coffee. Wouldn't say any more... "

Anna blew a long sigh from between pursed lips. How lucky she'd been that they'd been able to get their loan taken care of by the PCA. In desperation she'd gone on her own to get help from Morgan when Neil was sick with mono about ten years ago. "I guess I wouldn't be too surprised. We always suspected he was dishonest." She pressed her mouth into a thin line and shook her head. "Well, shall we get back to it?"

"Guess we'd better." Neil shaded his eyes against the sun and looked at a low, dark cloud forming on the horizon. "I think we might get some rain later. Better get as many of these bales up as we can. Sorry, hon," he added as Monica groaned.

They worked fast and furiously the rest of the afternoon, as the cloud spread and billowed closer, sending gusts of wind ahead to warn of the impending storm. As Neil dumped the last load of bales from that field, a streak of lightning flamed across the sky and a clap of thunder shook the air around them.

"Leave those bales," he shouted. "Get down off the stack."

The three of them clambered into the pickup as the first drops of rain splattered the dust, sending muddy rivulets across the windshield.

"Just in time." Neil grinned and gunned the truck toward home.

The rain continued through the night and next day. Anna swept and mopped and waxed the kitchen floor, vacuumed the carpets, and did the laundry. Neil and twelve-year-old Kevin puttered on the baler engine out in the shop. Monica worked on sewing her school wardrobe for her senior year, while eight-year-old Lizzie burned up the phone lines to all her friends. It was a much-needed respite from the heat and the hard work of haying.

When the sun came out again the following day, Anna and the three kids walked out to turn over the bales that had been left in the field. They had been soaked through, and now the side resting on the ground needed the air and sun to dry out again, so the hay wouldn't mold and rot in the stack.

"I gotta go into town tomorrow afternoon and play for Tim and Tina's wedding," Monica reminded her mother as they trudged across the field. "And on Saturday I've got three kids coming for piano lessons."

Anna nodded and smiled. Monica's musical talent was much sought after in the community, for weddings, funerals, luncheons and talent shows. And she always earned her Christmas shopping money by giving lessons to the grade-schoolers in the Horse Creek neighborhood. Anna could hold her head up high because of Monica's accomplishments. She no longer felt like hiding behind the canned goods aisle in the grocery store in Foster when she saw someone she knew. *Just let them say that Germans are dumb and our family hasn't achieved anything.*

"Evelyn is coming over tonight," she called out. "Do you kids want to make some music?"

"I s'pose," Monica answered.

"I gotta help Dad finish putting that baler engine back together," Kevin piped up.

Anna pressed her lips together. "Well, I'm sure your dad will want to get his fiddle out for a while too. It'll be fun."

Nothing from Lizzie. She was off chasing the dog, Fritzi, around the bales, crouching behind one and leaping out to tackle the collie when she came nosing around the corner.

All three kids were musically talented, taking after their dad. Anna fondly remembered the first time she had heard him play the fiddle. He didn't play much anymore, but would join in sometimes when their musically-inclined neighbors came to visit. Monica had tried giving her brother and sister piano lessons, but Kevin preferred to plunk on an old guitar he'd found at a second-hand shop. Lizzie caught on quickly, but she just wouldn't sit still long enough to listen or to practice. She preferred to clown around, to parody country western or popular singers she saw on TV. She sang seriously only when *she* wanted to.

Lizzie had joined 4-H but refused to take cooking or sewing projects. She wasn't interested in a horse or a steer, either. The cattleman's daughter chose to raise a sheep! Anna had thought Neil would swallow his tongue when Lizzie had announced her decision. Nothing they could say would talk her out of it. And now, she had to be continually reminded and prodded to take care of the animal.

"Oh, Lizzie, did you feed your lamb this morning?" Anna shouted across the field to get her younger daughter's attention.

"No, she didn't, Mom. I did. Again." Kevin's voice held a tone of disgust.

"All right, Lizzie, when we get these bales turned, I want you to go right home and do your chores. Do you hear me?"

"Okay, O-k-a-a-y," came the exasperated answer.

Anna sighed. Life with Lizzie was never easy.

~~~

Evelyn breezed into the kitchen, followed by fifteen-year-old Lana and a nice-looking, fresh-faced young cowboy. "Hey, everybody," Evelyn greeted, "I'd like you to meet my fiancé, Larry Sands."

Anna's mouth dropped open, and the dishtowel slipped from her fingers. It had been less than a year since Bud was killed.

Neil stepped from the living room and held out his hand. "Hi, there, Larry. Nice to meet you."

"Larry's riding for the T Bar J," Evelyn explained. She linked her arm in his and smiled up at him coquettishly. "Yeah, it was love at first bite, huh, honey?"

Larry mumbled something about "apple cobbler from heaven," ducked his head and grinned, a blush rising from his neck to his eyebrows.

"Well, that's great." Anna found her composure. "Go on into the living room and sit down. I'll bring coffee in just a minute." She leaned against the kitchen counter and looked at Monica's face, a mirror of astonishment.

"That was fast." Monica smiled.

Anna nodded. But Evelyn had been so lonely after Bud's death and craved companionship. She thought of her own fiancé, Fritz, who'd been killed in Germany during the war. It hadn't been too long after that she'd met Neil. She smiled. *Love doesn't operate on a time schedule.* Larry looked a bit younger, and it was probably a little quick, but then... if Evelyn was happy, who was she to judge?

"This calls for a celebration." Anna brought a bottle of wine into the living room along with the coffee and cookies.

As the men warmed up to each other and began to exchange horse and cattle stories, Evelyn beckoned Anna into the bedroom. She took a small package from her pocket. "Just a small token of my appreciation for your friendship, and for putting up with me all those months after the accident. You're a true friend."

Anna saw a liquid brightness in the other woman's eyes as Evelyn reached out to give her a hug. She opened the box to see an ivory cameo brooch and felt the sting in her own eyes.

~~~

When Anna heard Neil snoring softly beside her, she eased out of bed, took the small box from the dresser and went to sit in the rocker in the living room. By the silvery light of the full moon, she gazed at the brooch. It was one of the pieces of antique jewelry that Evelyn collected, and Anna knew it was one of her favorites. Her hands shook slightly as she caressed the exquisite carving.

Is this what it meant to have a friend? Something deep inside pinged like a tiny bell, something nebulous, yet like a spark piercing the darkness. Anna was jittery, as if she'd had too much coffee, but still there was something calming her soul.

"No. No." A voice echoed from the back of her brain. "Don't let yourself be sucked in. Remember what happened with Vickie... and those other neighbor women?"

She bit back tears. That was a long time ago. Perhaps she'd overreacted at times, allowed a perceived slight to become a giant obstacle. *I'm bigger than this. I'm not going to listen to these negative thoughts.*

Evelyn hadn't just taken Anna's help, her caring and her nurturing and then, in return, abandoned her. She had kept on coming to visit, to talk, to share... And Evelyn had brought her engagement news to the Mosers first...

Anna smiled. It was nice to have a friend.

CHAPTER EIGHT

Anna measured flour and sugar into a bowl for the cake she was baking and reached into the refrigerator for eggs. The container on the door was empty.

"Darn it." Lizzie had forgotten to gather the eggs—again. She marched to the door and yelled for her daughter. No answer. Grabbing a basket, she headed for the henhouse.

As she rounded the corner of the barn, she stopped and sniffed the air. Smoke. Then she caught a glimpse of a gray wisp curling up behind the chicken coop. She reached in the door, grabbed the chickens' water bucket and ran around the side of the building.

Lizzie, Kevin and Douglas Edwards were stomping on the remnants of a hay bale, trying to put out a small blaze. "Get back," Anna shouted and dumped the water bucket on the fire. It was enough to douse the flames. *Thank you, Lord.* It could been so much worse. An image of the prairie fire fifteen years ago flashed through her mind.

"How did this fire start? What is going on here?" As she turned, she saw Lizzie stuffing something into her back pocket. The boys stood back, sheepishly hanging their heads. "What did you just put into your pocket, Lizzie?"

"Nothing." The girl beamed her angelic face upward.

"Let me see it." Anna reached around her daughter and grabbed the pack of cigarettes from her jeans. "Lizzie, you are old enough to know better than this!"

Hands on her hips and mouth in a thin line, Anna faced the boys and glared. "Kevin and Douglas, I'm ashamed of you— you're almost thirteen years old. You guys could've burned the whole place down. Here you are, right next to the haystack and the barn."

66

She whirled toward her daughter. "Lizzie, get that basket I dropped by the door and gather the eggs, then go to your room." Anna waved her finger at Kevin. "You. Get in the house and start on your homework. And Douglas—on your bike. Go home. Now."

Her throat tight with fury, Anna spun on her heel and walked down the road to where Neil worked in the field. Her hands shook and her neck was flushed with fiery heat. What would she do with these kids? Not only was smoking bad for them, but the fire danger was sky high after the long, hot summer. What a close call. And Kevy with his asthma. She was sure Lizzie had instigated the episode, even though she was only nine. Douglas had probably brought the cigarettes since his dad smoked. Should she approach Carol Edwards with this? As in the past, Carol would probably defend her son and blame the other two, touching off another spell of the Edwardses not speaking to the Mosers. Anna bit the inside of her cheek. *Maybe I shouldn't mention it to her at all.*

By the time she reached the field, Anna had calmed considerably. "I need to talk to you," she said to Neil as he climbed off the tractor. She told him what had happened.

Neil's lips tightened. "Dadgummit." He shook his head and kicked at a clump of dirt. "Well, you know kids are bound to try tobacco sooner or later. But, starting that fire..." With a scowl he muttered, "Uh huh. I think just maybe those corrals need to be cleaned out again. They can start tomorrow as soon as they get home from school."

Anna trudged home, frustration and anger weighing her shoulders down. Where had she gone wrong with Lizzie? Perhaps she hadn't been strict enough with her youngest. Isn't that what people said—parents are the strictest with the oldest and by the time the last kid comes along, it's a spoiled brat. Maybe. But she couldn't see where she treated Lizzie any different from Monica and Kevin. Maybe she'd been too strict and Lizzie was just rebelling. No, Lizzie'd been a fussy baby. She'd been rebelling since she was taken from the womb.

Anna sighed. She would just have to keep a closer eye on that girl.

~~~

Late one blustery evening toward the end of January Neil answered the phone late to hear Jake's voice.

"I didn't want to worry you," his dad said, "but I thought maybe I should let you know I'm going into the hospital tomorrow for some tests. It's no big deal."

Neil's neck tightened and he took a quick breath. "Tests? What kind of tests?" Only a couple of weeks before, they'd been to Billings and stopped to visit Dad. He'd looked good, even had a lady friend, and they went out square dancing every Friday night....

"Oh, it's just a lung biopsy. They want to look at this emphysema. It's nothing. I'm fine. I'll be out in a day or two."

Lung biopsy. A chill ran through him. "All the same, I'm going to come in tomorrow, to see how you're doing." Neil put the phone down slowly, rubbed his hands through his hair and down the back of his neck before answering Anna's expectant look.

"Dad sure didn't say anything about having health problems when we were there. I know he's got emphysema, and he still smokes too much..." Neil sighed. "I'd better run in to Billings tomorrow."

~~~

The next morning Anna was down on her hands and knees scraping furiously at the old wax on the linoleum. Neil was right. Jake had looked so well and strong. She couldn't remember even studying emphysema in nurse's training. This must be something more serious—he hadn't shown any breathing difficulties. *And he goes square dancing every week...* She grabbed the scrub brush to attack the ugly space under the stove.

Anna jumped when the phone rang and bumped the mop bucket, sloshing water onto the floor. She glanced at the clock— just ten in the morning. What kind of news would this call bring?

"Hi, Mom, it's me." Monica's voice sounded weak and far away. "I'm not feeling so good. I guess I need to come home."

Anna sat. Oh no, not another one sick. "What's wrong?"

"Oh, I just ache all over. I tried to go to school this morning, but I just couldn't…"

"Do you have cramps?" She shifted in the chair. It wasn't like Monica to try to get out of school.

"No, it's a fever. Mrs. Dirning thinks it might be measles. A couple kids here came down with 'em."

A chill flooded through Anna. Measles at her age—that could be dangerous. "I'll be right in to pick you up, honey."

Anna threw a towel over the spilled water, jumped into the pickup, and sped into town. Trotting up the stairs to Monica's room, she found her daughter in bed, looking wan. She brushed her palm over Monica's warm forehead. "How do you feel, honey?"

"Not too good, Mommy." Monica's voice reverted to a little girl's tone.

"Come on, sweetheart. Let's get you home."

Monica sat huddled in a blanket all the way home, dozing and occasionally moaning. Anna gave her aspirin and orange juice and put her to bed. Then she went back to her scrubbing. It wasn't until after Kevin and Lizzie were home from school that Neil called.

"I'm going to stay in Billings overnight. I'm not sure what's going on here, but things don't look so good."

"Oh no. What…? Is he…?"

"I don't know. They did a full-fledged surgery. Nobody is telling me much. He doesn't seem to be doing very well."

"Oh goodness. Well, I'm sure the doctors have it all under control." Anna bit her lip, unable to think of any further reassurance. She told him of Monica's illness, and they talked a few more minutes before hanging up.

Anna sat with a thump. Her hands shook. Oh, dear, what now? She had never felt close to Jake. He'd always seemed to judge her, just like Papa... But still, Jake seriously ill... He was Neil's dad after all. She blinked away a rising tear.

"Mom, I'm hungry," Lizzie whined. "Can I have a cookie?"

"No. I'll fix supper now. Just wait a few minutes. Did you gather the eggs tonight?"

"Oh, Mom. Do I hafta?"

Anna pointed to the door. "Out."

~~~

She was running, running, running. Up the same hill. Over and over. She couldn't get to the top. Fear propelled her legs. Faster! Faster! Something was chasing her. She couldn't see it. But it was wailing. Groaning. Moaning...

Anna awoke with a start, her breathing fast and shallow. That old dream. She ran and ran and never got anywhere. Wiping sweat from her forehead, she lay back against the pillow. The moaning came again.

Monica. She jumped out of bed and ran into her daughter's room. The girl was thrashing around, tangled in sweat-soaked covers. "No. No. Don' wanna dance."

"Oh, honey, wake up. You're dreaming. Here, take a drink of water."

Monica drank, but didn't seem to wake up. She kept muttering. "Dance. President... Nixon. Dance. No."

Anna put her hand on Monica's forehead—*burning up.* She rushed to the bathroom, to fill a wash basin with cold water, and bathed her daughter's face and throat with a washcloth. Anna's stomach contracted with worry. *This must be the "hard" measles. I wonder if I should take her to the doctor?*

After a while Monica seemed to settle down, and stopped twitching and rolling her head from side to side. Anna sat on the bed beside her, holding her daughter's hand, stroking her hair and murmuring, "It's all right, honey. It's okay. I'm here with you."

Anna awoke with a stiff neck, her arm numb from falling asleep next to her daughter. Pale winter morning sunshine crept into the tiny room. Monica slept peacefully. Shaking the prickly feeling from one hand, Anna gently put her other palm on her daughter's forehead. *Ah, good, the fever is down. Thank God.* She shuffled back to her own bed for a few more winks. Thank goodness Kevin and Lizzie had both had measles already. She couldn't endure much more of this worry.

When she got up, Anna took Kevin and Lizzie to school, picked up the mail and a few cans of chicken noodle soup, and hurried back home. She peeked into Monica's room first.

"Hi, Mom." Her voice was weak, but cheerful, and her neck was speckled with bright red splotches.

"My, I see you *do* have the measles. Are you feeling better, sweetheart?"

"Yeah, I'm kind of hungry."

"I'll fix you some soup right away." She smoothed Monica's tousled hair back from her forehead. "Boy, you had quite a fever during the night. I was so worried about you."

"Oh, yeah. I remember dreaming. I was at a dance at school, and nobody was asking me to dance... except, yeah, now I remember—President Nixon—he asked me to dance. It was so weird. I kept saying no." Monica giggled, and Anna laughed with relief.

As Anna stirred the pan of soup and made tea and toast, she heard Neil drive up. She rushed to the door to welcome him. His white face and red eyes told her the news.

"Dad's gone... He never recovered from surgery..."

~~~

The winter weeks waxed and waned. Neil fell into a pattern of quiet desperation, spending long hours in the shop. Doing what, Anna didn't know. She found him one afternoon, one leg slung over the fender of the old truck he had been working on, a wrench dangling from his hand, just staring into nothingness.

She slid her arm around his shoulders. "You miss your folks, don't you?"

"Yeah." He nodded and sighed. "Y'know, it's just so strange. There was never a day in my life that Mom and Dad weren't there. Even when I was overseas, we kept in touch. And now, they're not. It was just so sudden, for both of them."

"At least you were there with your dad the last few days." She rubbed his arm gently, wishing she could soothe his anguish.

"But that didn't make it any easier, seeing him suffer." The lines in his face deepened and his voice rose. "Those doctors killed him. There was no reason to do the surgery that I could see." Neil smashed the wrench to the floor and stood up. "It's all so senseless." He trudged out of the shop, away from Anna, and headed up the hill where the machinery stood idle, waiting for spring.

Anna stood, helpless. The death of each parent had extinguished another spark in Neil. She felt a loss too, the loss of part of her husband. She hunched into her heavy winter coat and slogged through the snow, back to the warmth of the house. Why wouldn't he let her share his pain? He was drawing away....

The smell of yeast dough greeted her as she entered the kitchen, and she grabbed the big white dishpan from the top of the refrigerator where it had been rising. Anna drove her fist into the soft dough, collapsing its smooth round shape. Again and again she punched it, her tears adding salt to the bread.

~~~

Spring returned and the countdown began for Monica's last weeks of high school. Anna wanted to shout from the top of the highest hill when her daughter was named valedictorian and then

72

received the news she'd been accepted at the University of Montana in Missoula. Monica was giddy with excitement because of the journalism department's high reputation.

Anna shared her daughter's joy. But at the same time, a seed of dread grew inside. Her first-born, her little girl, all grown up, and ready to leave. She clung to her daughter on weekends, smothering her with all the love and affection she could muster.

"Mo-ther, for heaven's sake. Do you have to do everything for me? I'm eighteen years old—can't I have a few minutes to myself once in a while?"

The words were like a punch to the solar plexus. Anna sighed. She only wanted to spend as much time with her daughter as possible before she left.

Her hopes rose when a young farmer stopped by one day to talk to Neil. She saw his eyes grow wide as he took in the tall, slender blonde teenager with snapping blue eyes. The next Saturday, he returned and took Monica to lunch in Foster. The weekend following, he drove her the one hundred-ten miles to Lewistown for dinner and a movie. Anna clasped her hands over her chest. Maybe Monica would fall in love and decide to stay close.

On the other hand, Anna was frightened for her daughter, entering the dating world. Monica seemed to be friends with a boy at school who had taken her to important events, such as the Homecoming dance and the Junior and Senior Proms. But other than that, and going out a few times with that short cowboy who worked on the T Bar J ranch, she hadn't dated much during high school.

Anna paused as she scoured the bathtub. Her emotions seemed to be on a gravity-defying roller coaster ride. She and Neil wanted a better life for their children, wanted them to get a good education. She wanted Monica to learn, to follow her dream. And yet... she wanted her to stay right here, with her. Slumping heavily onto her knees, she gulped back sobs, afraid she would lose her daughter if Monica went away to college. That she probably would never come back home to stay.

Like Anna had done to her family. Had Mutti gone through that agony of losing her daughter?

~~~

"You know, your dad and I have been talking," Anna told Monica one spring day. "We think it's time I go back to Germany for a visit. Would you like to come with me? Just the two of us. It will be your graduation present." Besides seeing her family again for the first time in eight years, it would be an opportunity to spend time alone with her daughter.

"Oh wow, groovy! Yeah."

Anna made reservations for August, when the haying would be done. Monica took a bookkeeping job at the Horse Creek store for the month of June, to save money for the trip. Then she stayed home to help put up the hay crop. The young farmer kept calling.

"Honestly, Mom, I've got to go meet him this afternoon and tell him I don't want to go out with him anymore." Monica braced her fists on her hips and made a face. "I'm going to Germany next month, and then after that, I'll be away at school for four years. And who knows where I'll go after that? I really don't want any kind of commitment right now. It's just silly."

So much for my idea of them getting married and settling down close by. Anna hid her disappointment with a wry smile. "You're a smart girl."

~~~

Germany was lush and green and prosperous. With joyful tears, Anna held Papa and Mutti in a long embrace. They still looked healthy, although grayer and more stooped.

"*Ach, du lieber.*" Mutti kept shaking her head, smiling, and reaching out to touch Anna and Monica.

The cousins gathered around Monica, chattering at her in German, and she gamely tried to keep up, using what she'd learned in her rudimentary high school language classes. "Mom, I feel like a third-grader trying to communicate," she lamented at night. But Anna was pleased that the other young people swept her up and took her along on their dates and outings as though she'd been there all along.

Anna looked at all her plump relatives and listened to them recite their lists of possessions and how much each item had cost. At first she was a little envious of their beautiful houses with their oriental rugs and fine furniture, thinking this could have been hers, too. This is what she had given up to move to the "land of milk and honey." More like the land of drought and glaciers.

"Boy, everybody sure seems self-obsessed here," Monica remarked one afternoon after visiting yet another relative's fancy house.

Anna nodded. It didn't seem to matter how they came by their wealth and possessions as long as they had them. "I think it's because we had so little during the war. They're trying to make up for it now."

But she'd noticed, too. The attitude was different from the one she had developed living, working—and surviving—on the ranch. Smiling wryly, she thought of the filthy, cold shack they had moved into sixteen years ago and remembered her last visit to Germany when she'd deliberately not brought any pictures. Now she could proudly show photos of the bright, white-sided ranch house, surrounded by the Russian olive trees she had planted and the beds of pink, red, blue and white petunias in the front yard.

No one could say they weren't successful in America. She and Neil had started out with seventeen cows and now had a herd of nearly two hundred. And all of that had come from their own sacrifice and long hours of hard work, while enduring the heat of the summers and the frozen wasteland of the winters.

Anna looked at the pictures once again. Yes, she had done all that, right alongside her husband. They had made so much progress—together.

She loved spending this time with her daughter before she went so far away for college. And though she thoroughly enjoyed every minute of her visit, her thoughts often turned to Neil, Kevin, and Lizzie back home, and she was glad when it became time to leave. With bittersweet tears, she said good-bye once again to Mutti and Papa. Her heart contracted. Would she see them again?

~~~

The last weeks of summer were a whirlwind, getting clothes ready, notebooks purchased and necessities packed for Monica's dorm room at the University of Montana. Anna had little time to think about the fact that one member of the family would soon be missing.

Finally that long-awaited, sometimes-dreaded day arrived, and they drove Monica to Missoula. Anna and Neil helped her move into her room and unpack. She was happy to see a phone in the room. Then they met her roommate Suzi, a nice North Dakota Lutheran girl. Anna approved. *I can breathe easier knowing this girl will not be a bad influence on my daughter.*

She gave Monica a last, long hug. "Call us, honey, let us know how you're doing."

Her daughter grinned. "Okay, Mom. Don't worry. I'll be fine."

As Neil pulled the car away from the curb at the dorm, she slouched low in her seat, swallowing rising emotions. This was it. Her little girl was gone. They had prepared her the best they knew how, but it would never be the same. She felt as though she'd lost a friend. Kevin was his dad's shadow, and Lizzie… well, Lizzie was Lizzie—her own entity.

Monica was now living four hundred miles away from home. Sure, she'd been away during high school, but that was only thirty miles away, and she came home on weekends. Now she was in a strange town, among all these students and teachers with radical ideas. Would she stay true to herself? What kind of person would she turn out to be? Would she get into sex, drugs, and rock 'n' roll, as the song said? Surely, they had raised her to be stronger than that.

Retreating into silence, she nodded off as the miles rolled by. As long as she was asleep, she couldn't worry. But the empty feeling persisted after they got home and went about their daily lives once again—all made different now that Monica was not around. Neil still seemed withdrawn and didn't talk much about that absence that hovered like a living being. The sense of loss seared Anna's heart as severely as if her daughter were gone for good. Is this what people raised kids for—just to lose them? Sadness kept returning, and she pushed herself through the motions of daily living.

CHAPTER NINE

Anna reached out and tousled Kevin's curly brown hair. "My little Kevy, you've grown so tall and so handsome. Now you're going off to high school."

"Oh, Mom, please don't call me Kevy anymore." He snorted with disgust. "That's a baby name."

"Sorry, honey. I just remember you lying in your crib, so tiny and helpless—it seems like only yesterday."

Kevin rolled his eyes and turned to snap his suitcase shut.

"Did you pack the vitamins I gave you?" she persisted. "And that warm sweater, in case the evenings get cool?"

"Yeah, yeah, I got 'em. Don't worry about me, Mom. I'll be fine." He gave her a quick peck on the cheek and headed out the door to where the Edwardses were waiting to give him a ride to town.

Anna's lower lip trembled as she watched them drive away. Another baby bird gone from the nest. Only Lizzie left at home now. She turned to clear the breakfast dishes from the table. Lots to do. Gotta get these dishes done, scrub the floor, vacuum the carpet... No time to think.

By the end of the second week of school Anna sensed something different about Kevin when he came home for the weekend. He didn't talk about school and what he'd done during the week.

She put a hand on his arm and gazed into his face. "Something wrong?"

"Nope." He turned abruptly and went outside. He spent a lot of time doing chin-ups on the steel bar he had placed between the doorframes of the shop. The rest of the weekend, Kevin closed himself in his room.

A cold flutter of fear crowded Anna's thoughts. This was not like him. Her son had changed. And suddenly. While Monica was shy and quiet, and Lizzie the tempestuous, defiant one, Kevin had always been friendly and outgoing. He had always struck up an immediate conversation with visitors, was easy-going and got along well with his teachers and fellow students. And she thought she'd always had a good relationship with her son. But now... he wouldn't even talk to her. She couldn't reach him. Anna stood outside his bedroom door, with her hand raised to knock, then let it fall to her side and walked back to the kitchen.

She turned to Neil that night in bed. "Has Kevin said anything to you about school? Did something happen? He's so quiet, and that's not like him."

"No, he hasn't mentioned anything." He shook his head. "Going off to live away from home is hard, especially when you're not used to being around so many other kids. I remember it was quite an adjustment for me." He gave her a kiss on the cheek. "He'll be okay. Don't worry."

~~~

Kevin lay on his bed, trying to sleep. Only when he was asleep did the humiliation and hatred subside. He hated high school. It was like going to a foreign country. He hated all the kids, especially those smug juniors and seniors. All those rowdy guys punching at him and roughhousing—guys he didn't even know. Their taunts echoed inside his head.

"Hey there, farmer boy, did you lose your plow?"

"You a cowboy? Where's yer horse?"

"There's a specka straw in yer hair, ya hayseed."

"Mosey on home, Moser."

That second week of school, the school hosted an official initiation party for the freshmen. As usual, they were required to wear beanies with the school colors, orange and black, during the first two weeks of school. At the party, they were blindfolded, had a few innocuous pranks played on them, and then they danced.

The next day, as Kevin walked downtown after school, a red and white '56 Ford Fairlane screeched to a stop next to him. "Hey, Moser, where's your beanie?" called a senior.

"We don't have to wear 'em anymore." Kevin turned away and continued walking.

The doors of the Ford flew open, and four large, intimidating upper-classmen grabbed his arms and legs and dragged him to the car, kicking and flailing.

"Hey! Let me out. I don't have to go with you." Kevin fought the rising panic in his chest as the bigger boys crowded him in the back seat.

"Aw, c'mon, show us how manly ya are, cowboy. Here, have a drink with us." A burly kid Kevin knew as Frank shoved a whiskey bottle into his face.

"Hey, cut it—" Kevin's protest was cut off as Frank grabbed Kevin's chin and forced the neck of the bottle into his mouth, sloshing the bitter-tasting liquor down his throat and over his shirt. Kevin choked and struggled to free himself.

The car sped out of town, careening recklessly around corners, the speedometer reaching for the one hundred mark. The boys forced more whiskey down Kevin's throat. Fear drove him to twist and thrash. He tried to land a blow on his attackers, but they held him down and tore off his clothes. Helpless. He let out a guttural scream and head-butted Frank. Frank cursed. The driver slammed on the brakes, sliding the car sideways into a gravel pit off the highway. Yanking off Kevin's new cowboy boots, they shoved him out the car door with nothing on but his underpants.

"It's only ten miles back to town," one of the guys yelled as the car's tires spun a plume of gravel. "Ya better mosey on back, Moser." Their laughter and Frank's curses echoed as the Ford squealed onto the road.

The late September sun dipped behind the hill as Kevin trudged, barefoot, through the barrow pit beside the highway. His head spun from the whiskey. His feet stung from the gravel and sharp, dry weeds and grasses. *Have I gone to hell?* His face burned with humiliation. Fear still crawled through his guts. Would they come back for him? He tried to walk faster as he shivered in the crisp fall evening air. What would the old-time Indians have done? They survived without warm clothes and leather boots and automobiles. Ten miles wasn't so far. He'd walked that far many a time out in the hills on the ranch. But not barefoot. Not without clothes. Kevin wished for the teepee sweat lodge he had built when he was about ten. *Boy, that would feel good right about now.*

He concentrated on the memory of the hot, smoky fire inside the teepee and broke into a trot, ignoring the pain of his cut and blistering feet.

The whoosh of tires on pavement broke Kevin's concentration. He looked up to see a rust-spotted, dented white Chevy swerve to a stop nearby. His first thought was to dive into a culvert or a clump of tall weeds. He didn't want anybody to see him like this.

"Young man, are you all right? Do you need a ride?" A gray-haired, stoop-shouldered woman opened the car door, slowly eased herself from the driver's seat and shuffled to the side of the road. "Come here, dear, get in out of the cold."

He hesitated, but the woman motioned to him, then she half-turned toward the car. "Gail, get that coat outta the back seat for this young man 'fore he catches his death a cold." She handed Kevin a heavy old navy peacoat. "Here, put this on, and jump in the car, for heaven's sake. We'll give ya a lift into town."

Gratefully, Kevin pulled the coat over his nakedness, too miserable to be embarrassed, and climbed into the back seat of the old rattletrap, sharing the space with two large aluminum cream cans. A young girl of about ten, her brown hair in pigtails, peered over the back of the front seat.

"I'm Miz Fisher and this 'ere's my granddaughter, Gail," the old lady said, pushing her bulk back into the car seat. "Now, tell us, what happened to you?"

"Freshman initiation," he mumbled, now shivering violently.

"Well, ah'll be. Kids these days." The woman shook her head in disbelief. "That's why you ain't goin' to town school, Gail girl." She stabbed the air with an emphatic finger.

Miz Fisher dropped him off at the dorm. "Keep the coat, dear, and be careful."

Kevin tried to avoid the upper classmen after that and stayed in his room as much as possible after school. But even there, the older guys in the dorm tormented the freshmen boys, making them run errands for them and take over their duties at kitchen patrol and cleanup.

The only peaceful place was inside his mind, as he saw himself running, free, over the prairie, the wind lifting his moccasined feet and flapping his buckskin fringes.

~~~

Neil, Anna, and Lizzie sat in the bleachers, waiting for the basketball game to start. The Foster Mustangs were being challenged tonight by the Miles City Eagles. Kevin was on the "B-squad," which was playing a "warm-up" game before the main event.

"I hope he gets to play tonight." Anna put her hand on Neil's arm. "He was so disappointed last time when he didn't get out on the floor."

Neil nodded.

She craned her neck for a glimpse of the players. That's what happened when you lived out in the country. The kids didn't get the chance to participate in sports, and then when they got to high school, they were so far behind the town kids they rarely got to play.

"Ladies and gentlemen, your starting lineup," the announcer bellowed names as each boy ran out onto the court, "...Douglas Edwards... Kevin Moser..."

She stood with Neil, clapping and cheering. Kevin would get to play. Anna turned to smile at Carol Edwards, who was grinning ear-to-ear.

She beamed, too. Her little boy had grown up to be such a tall, handsome young man, and he was on the basketball team. That's what counted around here—basketball was *the* sport, and the entire county population looked up to the players. Football was just getting its start at Foster, and the team had yet to win a game.

"Go! Go! Yay, Kevin," Anna screamed as her son dribbled toward the basket. As he approached, he shot one-handed. The ball hit the backboard and bounced off. A Miles City player grabbed the ball and ran for the opposite court. Foster fans groaned as the other team made the basket. Parents nearby yelled out.

"Dang! Missed an easy lay-up."

"Get that Moser kid out. Put my Jimmy in!"

"Idiot coach! Why'd you put Moser in?"

Even Lizzie snorted. "Geez, Kevin stinks!"

Anna's shoulders drooped and her heart ached for Kevin. Oh, if only she could run out there and help him.

Kevin was back on the bench after halftime, and Anna unconsciously mirrored his dejected posture, reaching out to him with her eyes, her thoughts. *I love you, Kevin. I'm proud of you. You're a hero in my eyes.* She would try to tell him this after the game, but she knew that she would get little response. A shrug, a grunt, and he would shake her hand from his shoulder. She wanted so badly to gather him to her bosom, to comfort him, to take care of him and protect him as she had done when he was a baby. But she couldn't. She had lost her little boy.

~~~

Her arms reached out, stretching, grasping... The baby was falling... falling... into the black abyss... She couldn't reach him... Her fingertips brushed his blanket as the tiny body slipped away from her grasp....

Anna jerked awake. She blinked her eyes and shook her head to clear it. Such an awful dream. She shivered as she opened one eye and peered at the clock—four a.m. Tossing and turning, but unable to fall back to sleep, she was afraid she'd wake Neil, so she finally got up and padded out to the kitchen to make coffee. She sat at the table, held onto the warm cup with one hand and propped up her head with the other.

Neil found her like this at six o'clock, when he arose to do chores. "Couldn't sleep?" He rubbed her shoulder.

She shook her head. "I dreamed… I was holding a baby… and dropped it… into a black hole."

"Gee, I'm sorry, honey. Wish I could help." He reached under the sink to pull out the milk pail. "You've got to let go of them. There isn't anything you can do." He spread an upturned palm in a helpless gesture and headed for the barn.

That evening, they sat quietly in the living room after supper, Neil reading his news magazines and Anna darning socks. Lizzie was in her room, listening to LPs. The phone rang, splitting the peacefulness. "Ouch, darn it." Anna yelped as she poked her finger with the needle. "That stupid phone. What is it now?"

Neil picked up the receiver. "Yes, this is Neil Moser… Yes, he is… I see… Uh huh…" His voice tightened. "Okay, we'll be right in."

He sat heavily in the chair by the phone desk and clenched his fists. "Dangit."

"What? What is it?" She jumped to her feet, ran to her husband and shook his shoulders. "What's happened?"

"That was the sheriff. They've arrested Kevin at a kegger. He's in jail."

A strangled cry wrenched from her throat. "Oh, no." Her knees gave way and she sank to the floor.

Neil sighed heavily and put out a hand to help her up. "We'd better go in and get him."

~~~

Kevin lay in the back seat, pretending to sleep, his thoughts tormenting him. He'd done it now. The folks were really ticked off, not saying a word. Well, geez, couldn't a guy have any fun? The only way to have friends in this place was to go out drinking with them. What was wrong with that? He'd seen Mom and Dad drink a beer or a glass of wine once in a while.

His head spun and his mouth tasted of vomit. It wasn't really all that much fun, not the getting sick part anyway. But fitting in, living down the humiliation of his forced walk back to town... And not only that, but it seemed like every time he had gone into a class at the beginning of the year, each teacher had asked the same thing: "Moser, huh? Are you Monica's brother? You must be as smart as she was."

Ha! Fat chance. Monica was Miss Perfect, Miss Know-it-all, Miss Never-Got-in-Trouble. How could he live up to that? A hot tear squeezed from beneath his eyelid. Dang, he missed her anyway. She had been his ally against the bullies in grade school, never put him down, encouraged him. He'd always looked up to his big sister, wanted to be like her, be as good as she was... but he never would be.

The only way to get by at that school was to have lots of friends, and if that meant drinking a few beers... so what?

CHAPTER TEN

"... And now, to continue our twentieth annual Talent Show ... welcome our next musical group, 'The Psychedelic Cowpokes', with Lizzie Moser singing Janis Joplin's "Bobby McGee'..."

Kevin launched into the first chords on his electric guitar. Anna smiled. He seemed to be doing better, no more late-night calls from the sheriff.

The rest of the band followed, and Lizzie belted out the rock 'n' roll hit. Anna shook her head. Good heavens. How could a thirteen-year-old sound like Joplin? Must be those cigarettes. Her eighth-grade daughter already filled out the slinky sequined dress nicely as she gyrated and shimmied on stage.

She looked so grown up. Wonder where she got that dress? Anna sighed.

The audience cheered and stomped. "More, more," someone yelled.

"Thank you, thank you," Lizzie half-whispered in a sultry voice. "Come over to the community center after the show if you wanna hear more like this. We'll be playing a little rock, a little country..." She walked slowly up and down the stage as she talked, her dress shimmering in the spotlights. "We're gonna slow it down a little now with an oldie Linda Ronstadt remade, 'Silver Threads Among the Gold.' I want to dedicate this song to our mom, Mrs. Anna Moser, because I'm sure I've caused more than a few of those on her head..."

Anna sat motionless, too surprised to applaud. As Neil reached for her hand, she bit her lip, trying to keep the tears from coming. She looked at her husband and shook her head. Every time she thought Lizzie was a lost cause, she would redeem herself in a big and dramatic way. Anna could never stay mad at her youngest for long.

After the talent show was over, and the Psychedelic Cowpokes had won first place, Neil and Anna walked the few blocks in the soft early spring air to the Foster dance hall. "Lizzie sure is full of surprises." That eye-blinking speech still numbed her. "I didn't even know she sang in Kevin's band."

"I didn't either. But she's good." Neil's voice held more than a hint of pride. "I think she could have a career in music."

They sat, listening for a while, dancing to a slow, old familiar tune now and then. During a break Lizzie bounced up. "Hi, Mom, Dad. Enjoying?"

"Oh, honey, very much. You sang so beautifully at the show." Anna pulled her daughter close with one arm.

"You're quite the performer." Neil's grin gave away his pride.

"Thanks." Lizzie tossed her long, straight brown hair and fluttered her false eyelashes. "I'll be catching a ride home with Bonnie and her folks after the dance, okay?"

Anna hesitated. She hated the thought of leaving her daughter in town. She was only thirteen. But then, they knew Bonnie's family well. The girls had been best friends all through grade school. But before she could reply, Lizzie danced away.

Anna's face creased with concern. "I don't know about this." She looked around the hall for Bonnie's parents, but couldn't find them in the crowd. Finally, she spotted Bonnie's blonde hair in a tight circle of teenagers. Anna waved her over.

"Is it all right with your folks that Lizzie rides home with you?"

"Oh sure, yeah. They're groovy with it. Okay if she just stays overnight with me, then?"

"Well, I suppose so. But call us first thing in the morning and we'll come pick her up."

Bonnie waved at someone and was already halfway across the floor by the time Anna finished her sentence.

"You ready to head home?" Neil grinned. "This old fogie's getting tired."

~~~

Chores were done and breakfast long over when Kevin shuffled out of his room the next morning and plopped his lanky frame on the couch.

"Good dance?" Neil set his coffee cup on the end table.

"Yeah. They really liked our music."

"Did you see Lizzie leave last night?" Anna looked at the clock. It was eleven a.m. Her daughter should've called by now.

"Yeah. She left early—about midnight—with Bonnie."

Anna picked up the phone and dialed. Bonnie's mother answered.

"Are the girls up yet?" Anna asked.

There was a pause. "Uh… I thought… Didn't Bonnie stay over with you?"

Anna grimaced. What now? "No, they both told me Lizzie was going home with you folks."

Bonnie's mom uttered a low curse. "Those little vixens. I'll call around to some of Bonnie's friends. Let me know if you hear from her."

Anna hung up the phone, her hands shaking. "Neil, call the sheriff." She turned to Kevin. "Are you sure you saw them leave? Were they with anybody?"

Her son shrugged and shook his head. "She said she was going with Bonnie. I thought they had to leave the dance early to ride with her folks."

The call to the sheriff gleaned no information. "Well, at least she hasn't been arrested," Neil said.

Anna paced the living room floor. "Who else can we call? Kevin, help us out here. Where could she be?"

Neil spent the next hour on the phone, calling everyone Kevin could think of, but finding out nothing about Lizzie.

"I knew we shouldn't have left her." Anna held her hands to her hot cheeks, shaking her head, and walked from the living room into the kitchen and back again. She closed her eyes. *Oh dear Lord, what can I do?*

Just then a car horn sounded outside, and she ran to the window. A car full of teenagers pulled up, all waving and yelling as Lizzie and Bonnie jumped out.

Anna gave a little cry as warm relief flooded her. *She's okay!* Then the warmth turned hot and she trembled as anger boiled inside.

"'Bye. Thanks for the lift. See ya." The girls, giggling and shoving each other, tumbled into the house, hair flying, their eyes smudged with mascara.

Anna stood just inside the doorway, her feet apart, hands on hips, feeling a deep scowl etched into her face. "Where. Have. You. Been?" She forced each word between clenched teeth.

Lizzie stopped in mid-giggle and cocked her head to one side. "Oh, Mom, mellow out. We just went to a party at Patrick's house and missed our ride, so we crashed there. It's no big deal."

"No big deal?" Anna closed her eyes and willed herself to count to five before she spoke. "You lied. You both said you were going home with Bonnie's folks. No big deal? You are thirteen years old. You are too young to go to midnight parties. And, you should have called."

Shaking, she pointed a finger at her daughter. "You are grounded—forever! You are not to be in the band. You will not go to town without us. You will not be going to your eighth grade graduation dance. Do you understand? Now go to your room."

Lizzie's eyes blazed. "You can't do that! I hate you!" She spun on her heel.

Neil stood, his 6'4 frame towering dark over their daughter. "Don't you talk to your mother like that. She was worried sick about you."

Lizzie merely glowered at him and stomped off to her room.

Anna pressed her fingers to her throbbing temples and turned to Bonnie. "Go call your folks right now." She spoke firmly to keep her voice from shaking. "They are very concerned about you."

Bonnie's lips trembled, eyes wide in her ashen face. She nodded rapidly. "Okay." Her voice squeaked.

Anna sank into a kitchen chair, her whole body quivering.

~~~

The rest of the spring progressed without further incident. Lizzie dutifully stayed home, but dragged the phone with her and sulked in her room for hours.

Anna tried talking to her. "Honey, I know you think we're being hard on you. But we love you, and we don't want anything bad to happen to you. Do you know that?"

Lizzie sat silently on the edge of her bed, legs crossed, her foot kicking idly at the air.

"You look older than thirteen, and you feel older, and goodness, can you do a good Janis Joplin, but you are *not* an adult. And until you are, you will abide by our rules. And that means no smoking, no drinking, and no boys."

Lizzie rolled her eyes and stared at the ceiling.

Anna sighed. She thought her reaction as a concerned parent was reasonable, but she was simply lecturing to herself. "Okay, if you're not going to talk to me, I guess that is that." She turned on her heel and stalked out of the room.

~~~

Eighth grade graduation was held jointly with the Foster elementary students in an early evening ceremony, to be followed by a dance.

"Man, I feel like I'm carryin' a ball and chain," Lizzie muttered to Bonnie. "Everywhere I go, they're right behind me. I can't even sneak a smoke in peace."

"Yeah, me too. Major bummer. D'ya think you'll be able to talk 'em into letting you go to the dance?"

"No way. I've tried. They just don't dig it. I even tried to get Kevin to help me. If we lived in town, we could wait till they're asleep and then climb out the window or somethin', but it's kinda hard to sneak out when you live thirty miles out of town."

"Just wait till next year, when we're in the dorm. We'll have some fun then." Bonnie flipped her ironed-straight blond cascade of hair. "Oooh, who's that guy? He's *so* cute."

~ ~ ~

"We seem to have avoided a big battle over the graduation dance." Anna slipped off her dress and stockings late that night.

"It almost seems too good to be true," Neil agreed. "Surely she won't try to sneak out and go back to town now. We'd hear a car if anybody came to get her."

"Well, next is Monica's graduation in Missoula in two weeks. Maybe we can find a project for Lizzie to keep her busy until then." Anna leaned back against her pillow and closed her eyes, but sleep evaded her that night. She kept listening for Lizzie or a strange car.

She wondered if they would be able to let her live in the dorm next year. But what else could they do? Anna just couldn't move into town—there was too much work on the ranch for Neil to handle alone. Renting a house wasn't an option; there weren't that many available in Foster. Anna guessed they'd just have to hope that Kevin could keep an eye on her. At least the dorm had a curfew and Mrs. Dirning was pretty strict about the rules.

Anna nestled into her pillow, trying to get comfortable. She couldn't wait to see Monica and have her back home for the summer. Maybe she could get a teaching job around Horse Creek, and maybe she would take up with that young rancher again.

~ ~ ~

June 18, 1972 was bright and hot in Missoula, and the UM campus was filled with black-gowned graduates and their families dressed in their Sunday finest.

"You know my roommate, Jacki, of course." Monica greeted her parents as they came to her apartment. "And this is my boyfriend, Nate. He's in journalism, too. He'll be a senior."

Anna's eyebrows went up. Monica hadn't mentioned a boyfriend in her letters. That didn't sound good for her Horse Creek rancher idea.

"I got accepted into the student teaching program for fall quarter, so I'll come home this summer and help buck bales. I'll be back here in September and finish that up, and then I'll see what happens as far as a job goes," Monica told her parents.

So much for getting her to stay on the ranch. Anna's heart seemed to stop for a millisecond, but she simply smiled. "That's great, honey."

She sank onto the couch and watched the young people laugh and celebrate. Inside, her emotions ping-ponged. *But she seems to know what she wants.* Anna blinked back hot tears, missing her daughter already. Then she smiled as pride welled up, and she took a deep breath. Monica was a college graduate—the first one in the family to accomplish that milestone. *She will be fine.*

She raised her glass of lemonade. "Here's to the college graduates. Congratulations, all of you."

~~~

Anna reveled in having her children home for the summer. All three pitched in to work with the cattle, haying and harvesting, and that seemed to keep Lizzie out of trouble, but she still went into Foster every chance she got. Anna watched her leave with a helpless resignation, her chest aching, her arms heavy—nothing she did or said seemed to have any impact on her. It was as if Lizzie had divorced her family.

Monica soon made it clear that she wasn't the least bit interested in seeing the rancher again. She was moody and sat in her room, writing long letters every day to her boyfriend back in Missoula. Anna's suggestion to apply for a local teaching job didn't appeal to her at all.

Monica just waved her off. "We'll see. I want to do my student teaching first, and then see what happens."

The chasm widened between them.

And Kevin couldn't seem to recover his outgoing, open self. He didn't spend a lot of time at the ranch, either, heading off to Foster to practice with his band, or whatever... He wouldn't confide in Anna. She didn't know what he was thinking or feeling. All she'd wanted to do was shelter him from hurt, but she'd failed.

CHAPTER ELEVEN

Anna stared at the dirty breakfast dishes on the table. The silence slithered through the house. She could hear it, could feel its heavy hand on her shoulder. Neil was out in the field somewhere. Monica had gone back to Missoula to do her student teaching. Kevin and Lizzie were in Foster, Kevin a senior and Lizzie a freshman. Three times she had sent a child away to school, and three times that empty ache had filled her heart. She would never get used to it.

She had taken Kevin aside before school started. "You'll take care of your sister for me?"

He had looked at her like she was crazy. "Sure, Mom, I'll do my best." He shrugged and held his hands out, palms up. "But you know she dances to the beat of a different drum."

That's what Anna was afraid of. But she couldn't very well lock Lizzie in a room until she was twenty-one, although the thought had crossed her mind. She had done her best to instill values in her children, but she wondered if her teaching had just bounced off her youngest.

~~~

A heady sense of freedom had Lizzie floating. Here she was, out from under the old folks' prying eyes. Now, she could cut loose and have some serious fun. But, the dorm rules were pretty strict. She'd have to see what she could do to get around them. And worst of all, the legend of "Monica Moser" still echoed through the halls of Foster High. Yeegads, she hated her sister. A Goody Two-Shoes. Never got in trouble. Always got good grades. The teachers all loved her. And of course, Monica was Mom's favorite. Lizzie could never do anything right for her mother. *Mom must hate me because she can't control me like she does the others.*

Pffft! Lizzie snorted as she gazed into the mirror, checking for pimples. Monica. Little Miss Perfectionist was a wallflower. All she ever did in school was study. *She* never had any fun. Lizzie would show her. She'd show them all.

Monica and her friends had talked about going through a painful, shy, country-girl phase when they first went to high school. But Lizzie didn't know what they were talking about. So what if she was away from home, at a new school. This was heaven. Everyone wanted to be with her, even the town kids. Especially the boys. By the second day of high school, she had already drawn a group around her. They offered cigarettes, a ride in their cars, beer. *Take that, Miss Priss Monica.* She could pick and choose.

And she did. Every evening after dorm study hour, she had a date with someone new. She knew just how "far" to go, just how much to "put out" to keep them coming back, fawning and panting and giving her whatever she wanted—Cokes, ice cream, free booze, free weed. *Oh my gosh, the power!* It was intoxicating. And thank God, Kevin was ignoring her.

Tonight she was with Rob, a senior, the star forward on the basketball team. Lizzie leaned into the crook of his arm as they sat in his brand new black Barracuda, parked on "Blueberry Hill," overlooking the lights of Foster.

"Give me another toke of that weed," Lizzie said dreamily. "That's nice stuff. Where'd you get it?"

"A friend in Wynona has connections..." Rob inhaled deeply before handing her the joint.

~~~

Lizzie dribbled the ball across the court, looking for an opening. She faked to the right, but pivoted left and bounded through the hole in the defense toward the basket. Just as she set her foot for the throw, an elbow caught her in the eye. She went down, the pain dizzying.

"Robbie is *my* boyfriend," hissed a voice by her ear. "Stay away from him."

Lizzie jumped up, grabbed the other girl's hair, and gave a yank.

"Girls, GIRLS," yelled Coach Walters. "This is just practice. You don't have to get so rough. Save it for a real game." He knelt beside Lizzie, examining her right eye. "You'd better come into my office and lie down. I'll get you some ice."

Lizzie limped along next to him into the office, touching her puffy eye. She looked up at him, suddenly aware of how handsome he was.

"I'm sorry about your injuries. You have a lot of potential as a player." His forehead creased. "Girls play a lot dirtier than boys sometimes. I'll talk to Ronetta."

"Thanks." She gingerly touched the swelling. He was the only adult who understood.

The next afternoon Lizzie found Rob leaning against her locker. She smiled at him. "Hi, handsome."

"Hiya, doll." He looked down at his feet and scuffed at the worn wood floor. "Say, we're not going to be able to go out anymore. Ronetta and me, we been goin' out since sixth grade, and we're gettin' married in the spring. You know how it is."

Yeah, right, she knew how it was. Lizzie's gut tightened—he was good-looking and he was a senior. But she was used to dumping the boys. Now, she was being dumped. She put on a big smile. "Sure, handsome, I understand."

"But ... If ya want some more weed, just let me know, okay?"

"You bet I will!"

~~~

Anna knocked on Lizzie's door. "Can I come in?" With girls' basketball season underway, her daughter hadn't been coming home every weekend, and now that she was home for a couple of days, she just hid away in her room.

"Just a sec', Mom." After a pause, Lizzie opened the door. "Whatcha need?"

"I just want to talk to you awhile, honey. I've hardly seen you since you went away to high school, and I miss you."

"Oh." The teenager shoved a pile of clothes off her bed onto the floor and waved her mother toward the cleared spot.

A sweet, smoky odor pervaded the room. It didn't smell like cigarettes. Anna sniffed. "What's that smell?"

"Oh, just some incense. I like to burn some while I'm studying."

Anna looked around for the stick and saw the wisp of smoke rising from a ceramic jar. "Well, just be careful. You don't want to burn the house down." She smiled, as though joking. "You're not still smoking cigarettes, are you? You know how your dad and I feel about that."

Lizzie waved the question away. "Oh, Mom, lighten up. I'm fine. You worry too much."

But worry grew like a large, furry creature inside Anna as she left the room. She knew Lizzie did whatever she liked. And Kevin was stone silent. How was he doing, really? She couldn't tell. He was having a hard time in school, but she couldn't reach him. So much like Neil. Her husband mostly hid out in the shop—that was his way of dealing with problems. She missed him. Who was she supposed to talk to? Evelyn still stopped by to visit now and then, but not as often, now that she had remarried. And Anna sure couldn't confide her worries to someone outside the family. Although, Evelyn had told her that she put her daughter on birth control pills as soon as Lana started her period. Anna was shocked. She couldn't even talk to her daughters about *that* subject, let alone…

No, she was in this by herself.

~~~

Anna held Monica's letter in her hand.

...Student teaching is going okay, but I get so frustrated. I want to inspire each and every one of the kids to become straight-A students. But I know I can't do that as a student teacher. I only have two classes of thirty each. Regular teachers have five or six classes of thirty. How can we even make an impression?

She lowered the letter for a moment, happy that Monica would be completing her teaching degree. It would give her something to fall back on. Journalism was probably a glamorous-looking career, but would Monica really become a big-shot reporter? Or move to New York to work on a magazine? Anna couldn't see her doing that. Monica was much too shy. Besides, then she would never come home to settle down.

Anna continued reading:

Nate and I broke up. He seemed so jealous when I came home for the summer, but through his letters, I sensed something else was wrong. When I got back, he told me he thought <u>I</u> was getting too serious, that <u>he</u> wasn't ready for a commitment, yet. And we should start seeing other people. This was after I found out he'd already asked a girl from his reporting class to come to his apartment for dinner...

Anna sighed. Well, Monica wouldn't be marrying that one, at least. She saw Danny, that young farmer, at the store once in a while. Maybe she should let it slip that Monica was unattached again....

The next letter from her daughter read:

...You'll never believe this—Danny came all the way to Missoula bringing a huge bouquet of roses and a box of chocolates. I just about fell over.

Doesn't this guy get it? I'm just not interested. I told him, thank you very much, but I'm so snowed under with studies and teaching and thinking about a career that I'm not interested in a relationship. I think he was a little disappointed when I wouldn't go out to dinner with him....

Oh dear, so much for *that* idea. Poor Danny must be heartbroken. She read further:

I'm never getting married. Who needs the hassle? After Nate and I broke up, I started going out with this thirty-year-old guy I just found out is married!

Anna gasped. *Oh my gosh!* Her heart pounded. What if...? With shaking hands, she lowered the letter and sat with her head in her hands. The fear inside her thrashed and raked its claws. How was she supposed to protect her babies when they were all leaving her?

~~~

Life went on. In January, Monica called, with excitement in her voice, to say she had a job at the newspaper in Missoula. She would be doing layout on the society and religion pages and writing features for the Sunday edition. Now she had a real job and a paycheck. Anna smiled through tears.

CHAPTER TWELVE

Anna set the apple pie in the center of the table with a flourish, the fruit and cinnamon aroma wafting through the air. "Come now, Lizzie. Won't you have a piece of pie? It's fresh from the oven. I made it just for you."

Lizzie shook her head, not looking up from her plate. She had been pushing her steak, potatoes, and peas around for the past half hour. "I'm not hungry."

"Well, by golly, *I'll* have a big piece." Neil flashed her a hearty smile. "Kevin, would you get the ice cream out of the freezer?"

Kevin jumped up from the table. "Cut me a big slice, too, Mom, huh?"

"'Scuse me. Gotta go do my training run for basketball." Lizzie covered her plate with her napkin.

Anna frowned. "Right after eating? That's not good for the digestion."

Lizzie glowered, got up, took her plate out to the front porch, and set it in front of the dog who lay in the warm afternoon sun.

Anna watched her slip into her running shoes and take off up the hill.

"Well now, I know you both have to stay in good shape for basketball, but I sure don't see *you* running that much, Kevy. It just seems a little excessive." Anna shook her head and took a mouthful of pie and ice cream.

Kevin winced and shrugged. "Don't call me Kevy," he muttered.

Anna ignored his remark. "And she hardly eats a bite. Doesn't want to put on weight. She's just skin and bones to begin with. She oughta go visit Germany for a while. *Oma* would have some meat on her in no time."

Neil laughed. "Well, she does seem a little obsessed. But then, as long as she is breathing, eating and sleeping basketball, she's not getting into any trouble."

"I guess you're right," Anna had to admit, although she couldn't understand the teenagers of today wanting to stay so thin. Growing up during the war, she'd never had to worry about that. Only about getting enough to eat—and staying alive. Why, even now, back home, they weren't so concerned about being overweight, although most of the women she'd seen on her visits were a little over-plump. This younger generation would never understand what it had been like … not that she ever wanted her children to have to go through something like that.

Anna shook her head to clear her thoughts. "Anyone want another piece of pie?"

~~~

Lizzie ran and ran and ran. After the first half hour, she hit her stride and settled into a steady rhythm. The wind blew through her long straight hair, and she felt like she could go on like this, forever. Here, in the euphoric state of extreme exertion, she could forget everything else. Up the hill, down the steep sides of the coulee. In the pasture, the white-faced Herefords interrupted their placid grazing to turn their heads and stare at this human in a hurry.

It was an hour and a half before she made the circle back home. Now for weight training. She headed to the shop where Kevin had his chin-up bar and some dumbbells he'd made from old engine parts. Inhale… set… lift and exhale… Whoosh… Sixty-one, sixty-two, sixty-three…

The sun sank low over the rolling horizon when Dad and Kevin came into the shop. "Better knock off for a while, hon. Come on in for supper."

Lizzie continued to pull herself up on the bar, over and over.

"*I* probably wouldn't be able to do *that* many repetitions myself." Her dad looked down at his muscled, sinewy arms.

"Hey, c'mon, sis, Mom made pizza." Kevin picked up one of the dumbbells and did a few arm curls.

"Okay, I'll be done in a minute." Breathless, Lizzie pulled herself up again. She just had to make it to one hundred this time. She supposed she'd better go in and eat something, just to satisfy the folks. Mom was starting to get on her case. If the old lady had her way, Lizzie would be two hundred pounds and spend her days cooking and baking.

The thought gave her one last spurt of energy. "Ninety-nine… one hundred. I did it." She dropped down to the floor like a cat. "Okay, let's go eat pizza. Race ya to the house!"

~~~

Anna smiled at her family. It felt so good to have Lizzie and Kevin home for a weekend. And Lizzie was actually eating. Warmth rushed through her, and she reached out to squeeze both her children's arms.

"Great pizza, Mom. I'll have another slice." Lizzie grinned, holding out her plate. "You make the best."

The four of them laughed and talked through the meal as they hadn't for a long time. Oh, how Anna wished she could bottle this happy feeling and save it for the times when she was alone and longing for a hug, a smile, a teenage giggle. She formed a snapshot in her mind to take out and enjoy again later.

"That was wonderful, my dear." Neil pushed his chair back.

"Yeah, Mom. I'm stuffed." Kevin patted his stomach.

"Well, guess I'd better walk around the yard a couple times to work off all those calories." Lizzie jumped up and took her plate to the sink.

As her family finished up the dishes, still joking and laughing, Lizzie strolled outside, her hands pressed against her stomach. Okay, she'd done her "family duty" and ate with them.

Her shoulders slumped. Yeah, it was nice, it was fun, everyone was happy for a change, and no one was criticizing her. But she couldn't keep up the façade for long. Behind the barn, she doubled over, retching.

~~~

Anna felt like Neil could simply put the car in gear, close his eyes, and the Buick would know the way into Foster all by itself. With Kevin playing basketball and Lizzie involved in basketball and volleyball during the fall and winter, the new navy-blue Riviera burned up the seventy-mile round trip sometimes twice a week. Anna and Neil had agreed to take in as many games as possible, even though it sometimes felt like they were hardly ever home.

Kevin and Lizzie were good players and each made a fair number of points for their teams. The boys' team wasn't pulling out such a good winning record this year, but the girls were expecting to go on to the state tournament. Anna felt taller, slimmer, and more confident whenever someone congratulated her on the kids' accomplishments. Even when Carol Edwards delivered one of her backhanded compliments. "Well, I wish Dougie was as good as Kevin—maybe he'd get to play a little more often."

Both kids were still busy with their band, the "Psychedelic Cowpokes," and Kevin also played trumpet in the school band. Anna could literally see Neil's chest expand with pride at concerts as he watched his son play the same instrument he had enjoyed playing in high school. "That's my boy," he said almost under his breath.

As winter melted into spring, track replaced basketball. The kids went to more out-of-town meets, so Anna and Neil didn't have to travel as much, and they settled into their spring ranch chores.

~~~

"Psst! Hey, Rob!" Lizzie peeked around the corner of the older boy's locker as he deposited his books inside.

"Hiya. What's up?"

"Just wonderin' if ya got any more of that weed. I could sure use some after track practice. I get so sore." Lizzie grinned up at him and winked.

"Yeah, I'm gonna get some more tonight. My friend from Wynona is gonna be here. Why don'tcha meet us about seven out at 'the trees'?"

"Okay. I'll be there." She stopped in mid-turn. "Uh, is Ronetta...?"

"Naw, she isn't into that stuff. She'll be at some Junior Achievers meeting tonight anyhow."

Lizzie waved and bounced down the hall. She caught sight of Kevin going into the gym. "Hey, Kev."

He stopped, grinning when he saw her.

"Hey, you big, handsome brother of mine, can I borrow your truck tonight for a little while?"

"You don't have a driver's license yet, little sis, remember?"

"Pfft. Who cares? I've been drivin' since I was eight. Please? You know I'm a good driver." She looked up at him with pleading, innocent eyes. "I'm just goin' out to 'the trees' for maybe half an hour. I won't be drivin' in town, an' I'll be careful, an' I won't wreck it, I promise."

Kevin reached into his pocket for his keys. "Well, okay. But *be careful.* And I need it back by eight."

~~~

Lizzie drove sedately through the tiny town, trying not to catch anyone's attention, but when she hit the gravel road on the outskirts, she punched the gas pedal to the floor, making the light blue Chevy pickup buck and sway. "Faaaarrr out!" she screamed, her head out the window, hair catching the wind. This drivin' was almost as heady as good weed.

She skidded to a stop just past the turnoff to a small grove of cottonwood trees, the only such vegetation for miles. It was a landmark, and kids had been coming out here to party for years.

It was no secret, but the sheriff usually left them alone, as long as no one caused any trouble in town.

Lizzie jammed the pickup into reverse and sent a spray of gravel flying as she backed to turn onto the rutted lane that led into the grove. She could see Rob's Barracuda there already, and a bright red Mustang parked next to it.

"Hi, dizzy-Lizzie." Rob flung a long arm around her shoulders and planted a big kiss on her lips as she swung out of the pickup. It warmed her whole body, but she nonchalantly ducked from under his arm and walked toward the other boy.

"Hi, I'm Lizzie."

He was a short, somewhat pudgy teen, with dark hair—a little older than Rob. He finished a long drag on the joint and held his breath. Rob introduced them. "This is my friend, Hank, from Wynona. Hey, give *us* some Maryjane, all right?"

Lizzie took a toke, inhaled deeply, and felt her body slowly relax. The delicious euphoria filled her brain, crowding out all the negative thoughts. Only when she smoked this wonderful stuff did she forget about living up to her sister, being too fat, trying to win her mom's love, not being good enough, the other girls calling her a slut because all the boys were her friends.... Only now did she feel free, and happy, and loved.

~~~

Anna threw down the sock she was darning and stood up to answer the phone. "Why can't you just leave me in peace?" she muttered. "Hello," she snapped into the receiver.

"Mrs. Moser? This is Sheriff O'Reilly here in Foster."

Her heart threatened to jump out of her chest. She sat down hard in the chair next to the phone desk. "Y-yes? What's wrong?"

"Now, now. Nothin' serious. I just thought I'd let you know I stopped your daughter, Lizzie, tonight, drivin' without a license."

"Oh, no."

"An' I think she might've been smokin' a little marijuana. I could smell somethin' on her clothes, but she was actin' okay, so I let her off with a warnin'. Just wanted to tell you, so you can keep an eye on 'er."

"Oh. Okay. Yes, Sheriff. Thanks a lot." Anna slowly replaced the receiver and buried her face in her hands. Every time she thought things were going along smoothly, something new happened. Lizzie was always looking for trouble. Her puffed-up pride in Lizzie's sports prowess and singing talent was dashed to the ground when she did these things. *Why does Lizzie try to sabotage herself?*

She banged her fist on the desktop. She and Neil were doing everything they could to teach her right from wrong, to support her talents, and encourage her. But it apparently wasn't effective. What could she do different with this girl?

By the next day, the news had hit the grapevine. Carol Edwards called, and after chatting about the weather and inconsequential things, nonchalantly mentioned, "Oh, I heard Lizzie got into some marijuana."

All the blood seemed to drain from Anna's body. Now everybody would know about their family problems. She muttered something about "rumors" and hung up.

Drugs. She was gonna have to have a talk with Kevin—he was supposed to be watching out for her. What is Neil going to say—how do I tell him? Anna bit her lower lip, wondering what Mutti would do in a situation like this. *Probably "tan our hides" as Neil's dad would have said.* She smiled wryly. Lizzie was past that stage, and that would never have worked with her anyway. *How can I help her? Will she accept any help? Oh, dear Lord, I need your wisdom.*

Anna slumped over the desk and let the phone ring again and again without answering. It was as if the giant holding up her world had just stomped her into a wagon rut.

CHAPTER THIRTEEN

Kevin graduated from high school in the spring of 1973. He spent the summer at home, helping with the haying and harvest before setting off in his newly-acquired red VW bug for college in Missoula. With his parents' permission, he was going to stay with Monica and her roommate, Jacki. Lizzie was now a sophomore. Anna and Neil were down to one child.

Early in October, Monica phoned. "Just thought I'd better let you know. Kevin sold his VW, dropped out of school, and took off hitchhiking."

"What!" Anna's head swam, her knees weakened, and she sank into a chair. Her little boy, defenseless, off by himself, to who knows where?

"He called me from Houston last night, asking me to wire him some money. I guess he's working on the docks, but he didn't say much."

"*Ach, du lieber,* what now? I thought you were going to take care of him." Anna lashed out at Monica, then instantly regretted it. Her motherly fear made her heart run away from reason. What might happen to him? He can't cope by himself out there. She took a deep breath to calm herself.

"Mom. He's eighteen years old. I'm not his baby sitter," Monica protested. "He wasn't happy in school. I tried to talk to him, but you know how quiet he is. Never says much. I don't know what the problem was. But don't blame me." She hung up abruptly, leaving Anna with the receiver still glued to her ear.

When Neil came in at noon, she was still sitting at the kitchen table, her little finger tracing the paisley swirls in the plastic tablecloth.

"Oh, boy. What is it, honey?" He sat next to her, folding his big hands around one of hers.

"Oh, Neil." She peered up at him and blinked back tears. "Kevin quit school, and then hitchhiked to Texas. I'm so worried about him. What are we to do?"

Neil sighed deeply and stroked Anna's hand with a soothing, gentle touch. "Don't be so worried. Kevin'll be okay. He's a big boy now, a man, really. He can take care of himself. I wasn't much older when I went off to the army."

Anna pictured the mature, strong young man she'd met in Germany after the war. Kevin was a lot like his dad, but Anna couldn't help herself. It seemed she was born to worry. He was her only son. She simply wanted to protect him from the heartache the world could bring him. *Please, God, take care of him.*

From then on, she threw herself into ranch chores and kept the house spotless, working constantly, from sun-up to sundown—anything to keep from thinking.

Lizzie's basketball games soon put Anna and Neil on the road again. Anna was glad for a diversion and cheered as loud as she could for her daughter.

~ ~ ~

"Lizzie Moser—phone call!" someone yelled up to the second floor from the dorm lobby. Lizzie skipped down the stairs to take the call.

"Hi, this is Hank. You wanna meet me? Same place?"

"Uh… hi, Hank. Sure. Just got outta school. Can you pick me up in fifteen minutes—outside the dorm, though? I don't have any wheels."

Hank had been calling every couple of weeks since Rob introduced them. They usually met at "the trees," and spent a blissful evening rolling doobies and smoking. She never asked his last name, and neither of them talked much when they got together. He wasn't her "type" to date, and the only thing he could offer that interested her was the marijuana.

"I got somethin' special today," he greeted as she slipped into his red Mustang.

"Good. I could use some cheering up. Mom's really on my case at home about my eating, and coach is bugging me about my grades. Why should *they* care? As long as I pass all my classes and make lots of points every game..." Lizzie slumped heavily into the soft seat and stared out of the window.

At "the trees," they sank down behind a fallen log and lit up. "Wanna try this new stuff?" Hank held out a small pill. "It's called 'acid,' and it's prime. It's a real trip, you've never had such a far-out groove. Like Uncle Timothy Leary says, 'Tune in, turn on and drop out.'"

"Sure, what the heck. I'll try anything once." She popped the pill into her mouth and washed it down with a swig of beer. If she put enough of this into her head, maybe all the scary stuff inside would be squeezed out....

They sat quietly for some time. Hank flipped on a transistor radio and Pink Floyd's "Brain Damage" from *Dark Side of the Moon* echoed from the tiny speaker. He inhaled his weed deeply and popped open another beer. Lizzie closed her eyes and pinwheels of color swirled behind her eyelids. Circles ebbed into waves of brilliant sensation, and she floated above the earth. Opening her eyes, she saw the grove of trees as a splash of bright oranges, yellows and reds across an ocean of blue. She squinted and the kaleidoscope narrowed until she could see the veins of a leaf pulsating with light and heat. She danced with the trees. She felt like she could fly. She laughed and screamed and cried with the great joy that burst from her heart.

It was dark when she at last came back to some semblance of reality, opened her eyes and saw Hank calmly sitting there, still smoking and drinking. Lizzie smiled and stretched languorously. "Wow. Was that ever far out. You were right. I *like* this stuff."

~~~

Half-way through basketball practice, Lizzie's head reeled. She dropped the ball and bent her head toward her knees. When her vision cleared, she saw Coach Walters come out onto the floor. She waved him off. "I'm fine. Just got a little dizzy for a minute." She trotted off for the next play.

But when she opened her eyes again, she was lying on the gym floor, her teammates in a ring staring down at her. The coach bathed her face with cold water and held smelling salts to her nose. Lizzie coughed and tried to sit up.

"No, no. Stay down. I don't want you to play anymore today." The coach looked at the rest of the team. "Okay, girls, the rest of you run laps till the end of the period."

After everyone had gone, Walters stayed behind, sitting on the bench with Lizzie. "You fainted, Lizzie. When did you eat last?"

She shrugged. "I dunno. I'm fine, Coach, really I am. I gotta do my laps now."

"No, you don't need to do laps today. C'mon, I'm going to take you downtown for a burger and a shake."

Lizzie's stomach roiled, and she ignored the hamburger, but out of duty she sipped at her chocolate shake and nibbled at the French fries. "Why are you making me do this? I'll get so fat I won't be able to play basketball if I eat like this."

Walters peered at her over his glasses, concern etched on his face. "Well, you won't be able to play either, if you waste away to nothing. Lizzie, you're too thin. You're getting weak. You need food for fuel."

She grimaced at him.

"No, kiddo, I mean it. You're my star player. I can't afford to have you get sick. And, I care about you."

Lizzie's throat suddenly closed up, and her eyes stung. She didn't dare meet his eyes. She drew patterns in the ketchup with a fry, trying to swallow whatever was stuck in her throat.

"Are you having trouble at home? In the dorm? Can you talk to me?" His voice was soft and soothing.

110

"Oh, Coach, you're the only one who cares." She gazed up, her eyes suddenly flowing, her face red. Holding her napkin to her mouth, Lizzie slid out of the booth and ran from the restaurant.

~~~

Anna eagerly ripped open the envelope with the Missoula return address. She so much looked forward to these letters. She only wished Monica lived closer so she could experience her oldest daughter's accomplishments and share her life's journey with her.

Dear Mom, Dad and Brat,

Anna rolled her eyes. Why did Monica still call Lizzie that after all this time? She chuckled. *I guess it still fits.* She went back to the letter.

Thought I'd drop you a line and let you know I'm coming home for a visit at Thanksgiving. I'll be bringing a friend. Everything's going fine here. See you then.
Love, Monica

Bringing a "friend," huh? That could mean only one thing— a boyfriend. Anna knew Monica's roommate, Jacki, and had met several of her other friends. It couldn't be one of them or Monica would've said so. Surely she wouldn't spring an engagement on them. No, that couldn't be it.

Anna made a quick inspection around the house—better get this place cleaned up, start baking some pies, get a turkey…

~~~

The day before Thanksgiving, snow drifted down lazily all day, adding depth to the foot of white stuff that had already fallen the night before. Anna fretted about Monica and her friend traveling 400 miles over those roads.

Lizzie had just come home from Foster, catching a ride with Bonnie's parents. "The roads are slicker than hog-snot," she announced with pessimistic exaggeration. "They'll never make it tonight."

"Don't say that," snapped Anna. "I'm worried enough already." She smoothed imaginary wrinkles from the tablecloth and counted the place settings for the umpteenth time. How she wished Kevin were coming, too. What had possessed him to quit school and go off to Texas? She went to the sink and stared out of the window through the swirling snow, up the road and toward the Horse Creek store. "Oh, I think I see a light on the road. It must be them."

Neil and Lizzie joined her at the window.

"Yep. It's turning onto our road." Neil turned and headed toward the porch. "Make sure the yard light is on, Lizzie. I'd better get my overshoes on and help them bring in their things."

Anna turned on the burner under a pot of water for spaghetti, and stirred the sauce. After a few minutes, the dog barked sharply, and she heard the outer door to the porch open, feet stomping off snow. She ran to the kitchen door. "Oh, honey, you're here. We were so worried." She hugged her daughter, then held her at arm's length. "Let me look at you. My, it's good to have you here safe and sound."

"Hi, Mom. The roads were okay most of the way. We didn't have any trouble." Monica hugged Anna and then stepped back. "Mom, Dad, Lizzie, I'd like you to meet my friend, Tom Davis."

Tom's handshake was firm. "Great to meet you, Mrs. Moser, Mr. Moser. Hi, Lizzie."

"Oh, just call us Anna and Neil." She smiled. Exactly as she'd thought—a boyfriend. Her stomach fluttered. "Bring in your stuff. Monica, show Tom to Kevin's room." Everyone scattered to get settled in, and she put final touches on the meal.

During supper, she studied this young man Monica had brought home. He stood an easy six feet, blessedly taller than her tall daughter, but still appearing short next to Neil. He had neatly trimmed, straight brown hair, a mustache, and mischievous hazel eyes behind thick glasses. He was a fast-draw with a joke, quickly putting the Mosers at ease.

Anna saw the way Tom looked at her daughter. She could see that he was head over heels in love with her, but wondered if Monica knew it yet. She chuckled to herself. The girl who only a few months ago declared herself through with men. But then the butterflies in her stomach reminded her that this man lived in Missoula. He was a salesman, not a rancher. Would he take her daughter away from her?

She tried to harden her thoughts toward him, but found herself laughing at his humor and enjoying the teasing and the gentlemanly way he treated the three women.

Thanksgiving, with most of her family together again, was a warm, delicious treat. The food turned out perfectly, and even Lizzie ate heartily. The festivity had one hole in it though—no Kevin. He had called from Houston. He was okay, he assured her, just wasn't into the school scene right now, wanted to work for a while. But he wasn't going to be home for the Christmas holidays, either. She took a deep breath, trying to fill the hollow place in her chest, and turned her attention back to the family around her. Gradually, the laughter and gentle camaraderie lifted her above the worry about her missing son.

When she couldn't coerce her charges with another bite of pie, they all pushed themselves from the table. Neil moaned. "Wonderful meal, honey."

Monica stood and gave her a hug. "That really hit the spot, Mom."

"Well, now you're going to be walking around with a bruised spot," Tom quipped.

Anna stared at him for a moment. Then she chuckled as Monica giggled and cuffed his shoulder.

Tom asked if she and Neil minded if he turned on the football games.

Anna paused. Football? On Thanksgiving? That wasn't a Moser family tradition. Nobody in the family was interested in football. She frowned. "Well... I don't... Football, huh?" But then she smiled at his crestfallen face. "Oh sure, help yourself."

He and Neil retired to the living room to watch the game.

Lizzie stacked the plates and carried them to the sink. Suddenly she clutched her stomach and ran toward the bathroom. Alarmed, Anna followed her to the door, where she heard her vomiting. "Lizzie, are you all right?"

Finally she heard water running, and the girl came back to the kitchen where Monica was washing dishes, her face ashen. "Lizzie, honey, are you sick?" Anna reached out to gently touch her daughter's forehead.

She pushed her hand away. "I'm okay, Mom. Just ate too much pie. I'll be fine now."

Monica gazed at her sister through slitted eyelids as she swirled the soapy dishwater. "Have you had this problem before, when you eat?"

Lizzie scowled. "No! I'm fine. Shut up, Miss Perfect! It's none of your business." Her voice rose. "Will everybody quit worrying about me? I just ate too much, all right?" She stalked to the kitchen door and slammed out into the entry porch.

"Mom, she's skin and bones. Something's wrong."

Anna smiled and waved a hand as she grabbed a dishtowel. "Oh, I think she's all right. She's so conscious of keeping in shape for basketball, that's all."

"Well, I don't know. I've heard about this new thing at college. Girls think they're fat, no matter how skinny they get, and refuse to eat. Or they stuff themselves with huge amounts of food and then throw up on purpose. I think you'd better keep an eye on Lizzie."

Anna's breath caught in her throat. "Oh, that's horrible. Well, I have been a little worried about her," she admitted. That couldn't be... Not *her* baby...

~~~

Later, Monica went into Lizzie's room. "Hey, how's things?"

Her sister shrugged. "Okay." She sat cross-legged and picked at the fringe on her bedspread.

"School goin' all right?"

"Fine."

"I hear you're doing really good in basketball."

"Yeah."

"Have a boyfriend yet?" Monica glanced at their reflection in the mirror and took a deep breath. This was a rather one-sided conversation. Her heart ached. But she didn't know how to draw her sister out.

"Not really."

"Liz…" She swallowed. "Do you think you're fat?"

Her sister shot her a look of pure hatred and snorted. "What do *you* know about it, Miss Priss? You don't have to rely on your looks to get what you want. You're naturally perfect. You've always been Mom's favorite. I was just the accident in the family. So don't bug me, okay?" She threw herself flat on the bed, facing the wall.

Monica's breath caught in her throat, and she stared dumbfounded at her sister's back. "No, none of that is true. I'm not Mom's favorite." Her hand trembled, wanting to comfort her. *How can I reach her?* "I don't have life perfected. I've always been shy. You don't remember, but kids bullied me when I was young." She blinked back a tear. How did Lizzie come to dislike herself so much and hate her family? "You are very outgoing and everyone likes you." Monica put a gentle hand on her sister's shoulder. "Hey," she said softly. "Mom loves you. We *all* love you."

"Leave me alone. Get out," Lizzie snarled and violently shrugged off her hand.

Monica bit her trembling lip, slipped off the bed, and left the room, quietly closing the door behind her. She leaned against it for a moment. *Oh my gosh. She really does have problems.*

~~~

Coach Walters called a couple of weeks later. "Mrs. Moser, Lizzie fainted at basketball practice, and we took her to the hospital this afternoon. This isn't the first time. It's happened several times, and I'm concerned about her. Doc Farnum is, too. He'd like to keep her there a day or two for observation."

"Oh my gosh. We'll come right in." *The hospital. What now with this girl?* Anna's heart pounded, and her hands shook as she went to find Neil. *Ach du lieber.* She should've been able to protect her little girl better.

Yet another hurried trip into Foster. The coach met Neil and Anna in the hospital lobby. "I've been kinda worried about her. She doesn't seem to eat enough, and she's obsessed with exercising and training for basketball. I'm sorry I didn't call you about the problem sooner, but I didn't want to alarm you. Have you noticed anything at home?"

Anna nodded. "I think she's way too thin, but she seems to eat when she's at home. Our older daughter, Monica, told me about some girls at college who starve themselves…"

"I think Monica hit the nail right on the head." Doc Farnum came up behind them, putting out his hand to shake Neil's. "It seems to be something new that girls are getting into. All the movie stars are so thin these days, and the teens want to look beautiful and glamorous, just like them."

Coach Walters nodded and slouched against the wall.

Anna frowned. These young girls were all so slim and pretty already. To her, natural beauty always trumped a lot of make-up and fancy clothes.

The doctor took his pipe out of his jacket pocket, scraped the tobacco out of the bowl into a wastebasket nearby, and refilled it. The pungent, spicy odor filled the space around him, momentarily drowning out the antiseptic hospital smells.

Anna watched with abstract fascination, thoughts about Lizzie and movie stars and not eating whirling through her mind.

116

What had she missed along the way? Was it something she could have prevented? If only she'd known…

Striking a match and taking a long, thoughtful puff, Doc finally continued. "Now, I'm not a psychologist, but from my reading about this issue, it seems these girls are constantly striving for perfection, feeling they fall short of expectations."

"Perfection?" Anna humphed. "I've never been able to get her to do anything the right way her entire life. That's nonsense." She sighed and turned to Neil with a helpless shrug. Papa's words echoed in her mind, "When you do something, do it right." Her breath hitched. She never felt she could measure up to Papa's standards. *Oh dear.* Tears welled up.

"It's okay, honey." Neil's brow furrowed, and he put an arm around her shoulders.

"Perfectionism is the enemy of good enough." The coach's voice came from behind them.

Anna turned toward him, frowning. "What?"

"A quote from Voltaire." He smiled. "I teach history too. Anyway, I see that perfectionism has two faces. One is actually striving to do everything perfect, never stopping until it is, and the other is to quit or not try something if you can't do it perfectly the first time."

She blinked. She could see both of those in herself.

Neil squeezed her shoulder. "What can we do, Doc?"

The doctor puffed on his pipe again. "Well, it's going to take some patience. She's going to have to be in the hospital for a while, to get her built back up physically."

Anna had dealt with the wounded during the war, Monica's polio, Neil's mono, and Kevin's various scrapes, bumps, and bruises. But this was something entirely out of her realm of understanding. She'd never heard of such a thing—these new theories about perfection and not eating. Where did that come from? "Can we go in and see her now?"

Doc Farnum nodded. "So far, she hasn't talked to anybody but Coach Walters, here. But I'll let you come in, one at a time, just for a minute."

"She was a little PO'ed at me at first for bringing her to the hospital, but I think we're getting past that now." The coach straightened his stance and motioned down the hall. "Good luck."

Anna stepped into Lizzie's hospital room, tiptoeing, in case she was sleeping. She stopped at the sight of the intravenous tubes running to her daughter's arm. *Ach, du lieber*, it really *was* serious. Her knees turned to gelatin, and she sat heavily in the chair by the bed.

Lizzie opened her eyes, saw who her visitor was, and turned her face away.

"Are you feeling better, honey?"

A snort. "Never felt bad."

"Well, sweetheart, fainting isn't exactly the picture of robust health. And if your coach and the doctor both think there's something wrong…"

"Nothing's wrong."

"Lizzie, can you tell me what's bothering you? I want to help. Please. Don't you know I love you?" Tears came to Anna's eyes and her throat constricted.

A strangled howl of anguish came from the wraith in the bed. Lizzie turned her head to direct a piercing, malevolent look at Anna. "Love me? You don't *love* me. I never did anything right for you. You love Monica and Kevin, but you *never* wanted me." Lizzie jerked up on one elbow, her face twisted. "I hate you! Get out! I hate you! I hate you!"

The fear-beast in Anna's stomach churned and grabbed her heart, strangling her. She stood up, knocking the chair to the floor, staring at this daughter so filled with anger and hate. Rushing from the room, she jammed a fist into her mouth to contain her screams. Tears blinded her. Could it be? Realization struck her dumb. Had *she* caused this illness? Oh dear God, what had she done?

She stumbled to the door, running headlong into Doc Farnum. He patted her shoulder. "It's all right, Mrs. Moser. Come with me."

Still holding her hands over her mouth, tears streaming from her eyes, Anna shook her head. "It's not all right." Her neck and face burned. He'd overheard Lizzie's tirade. What must he think?

The doctor drew her into the crook of his arm and led her to the waiting room where Neil sat.

"*Liebchen*, what happened?" He rose to steer her into a chair.

"She hates me. She thinks I don't love her." Anna buried her face in her hands. Was God punishing her now for feeling resentful of her willful daughter who had been trouble since the womb? The darkness of depression descended.

CHAPTER FOURTEEN

Anna sat at the kitchen table, thoughts chasing each other around until she could have screamed. Her Lizzie so sick. She looked at Neil.

"It hit me over the head like a two-by-four." Anna blinked, trying to ease the dry puffiness. "The doc said these girls with this eating problem are obsessed with perfectionism. And my first reaction is, she's never done a thing the right way in her life."

He stabbed at a piece of pie and pushed it around his plate, a slight shrug lifted his shoulders.

Anna rubbed her hands together. "Well, maybe my expectations were too high. Maybe she felt like I expected her to be as good as Monica."

"I don't understand this concept." He seemed to sink deeper into his chair.

"All I wanted to do was teach my children to strive for their best. I just wanted them to overcome this darned... this... *prejudice* that everybody here has against our family... because of the war against Germany. I only wanted my kids to have what I never had." Anna broke into tears again. "And she hates me for it." *How can a daughter hate her mother?*

Neil reached out to touch her arm gently. "Oh, I don't think that's necessarily true."

Not necessarily? She wiped the tears from her cheeks. Did Neil really not understand how prejudice had affected her, probably even her relationship with her children? "Sure seems like it. What on earth is this starvation stuff, anyway? She's a country girl, from a good family. How would she ever have gotten these ideas?"

Neil shook his head and sipped his coffee. "I don't know. I've never heard of such a thing. Maybe going to school in Foster has been a bad influence on her."

"Do you really think so?" A knot loosened in Anna's stomach. Maybe it wasn't *all* her fault. "But what's the alternative?" She felt so helpless. "We certainly couldn't send her somewhere farther away. Besides, we were losing control over her as it was. What are we going to do?"

Not only did Lizzie consume her thoughts, but Anna's insides churned with worry about Kevin—wandering around out there all by himself, no one to take care of him. "And Kevy. What if he isn't eating right? Not dressing warm enough? What if he gets sick? Is he working? Making enough money to live on? What if he gets in with the wrong kind of people?"

Neil put his hand on her arm. "I know, sweetheart. I worry about him too. But we have to let the kids go—they're growing up. We can go in and talk to Doc again tomorrow about Lizzie. And maybe Coach Walters, since he's the only one she seems to relate to. There's nothing more we can do now. Let's just pray and ask for the wisdom to deal with this."

Anna nodded. At least Monica was stable and down to earth. They could always rely on her....

Later that afternoon, Anna studied her Christmas card list. She glanced up at the calendar. December 11, 1973—that's right. Yesterday was Monica's birthday. *Wonder if she got the package in time?* Her first baby—twenty-four years old, now. *Oh goodness, that means I'll turn fifty in February.* Where did all those years go? She stared at the pile of cards and thought back to her arrival in America in 1948. Boy, was she optimistic and naive, then.

She jumped as the phone shrilled on the desk beside her. Pesky thing.

"Hi, Mom, it's Monica."

"Oh, hello, dear. I'm so glad you called. I was just thinking of you. Did you get my package?"

"Yeah, thanks. The chocolate cake arrived in perfect condition. Packing it in popcorn was a great idea! And thanks for the sweater—it's gorgeous."

"Well, how was your birthday? Did you have a party, or did you go out?"

"Tom took me out to dinner at the Edgewater Restaurant. We had lobster and champagne and danced. It was so much fun." Monica's voice was dreamy. She paused. "Mom… Tom asked me to marry him… and I said yes."

Anna's mouth opened, but no sound came out. Monica was waiting for a reply, but finding the right words was so difficult. She couldn't bear the thought of her little tow-headed girl all grown up, getting married, being with a man.

Finally, a word popped out. "Wow." It was flat, she knew, devoid of excitement. But how could she be enthusiastic when her daughter was being taken away—forever?

"Well, don't worry, Mom. We're not rushing into anything. We probably won't get married for two or three years." Her voice was soft, with a hint of disappointment. "Anyway, how is Lizzie doing?"

Anna filled her in, and after a few more minutes of small talk, they ended the conversation.

Anna sat for a long time after she hung up. She should've seen this coming, after watching them together at Thanksgiving. Yet, somehow she thought Monica would stick to her guns, like she had with that young rancher. Darn, marrying the local boy would have been so perfect.

~~~

The next day, Anna sat next to Neil in the hospital cafeteria with Coach Walters and Doc Farnum. Again, Lizzie had refused to talk to them, just turned her face to the wall and seemed to ignore what they said. All Anna could do was tell her again that she loved her. An overwhelming sense of sadness settled like fog into every crevice of her being.

"We had a pretty good talk yesterday," Walters said. "I'm just kind of flying by the seat of my pants here, but she seems to trust me. So far, anyway."

"Do you have any clues to why this all happened?" Neil looked from Walters to the doctor.

"It's all pretty complicated," Doc said.

The coach spoke up. "She told me about feeling like she had to live up to her older sister's image. That she feels you love Monica best, and you love Kevin more than her just because he's a boy. She thinks you never wanted her to be born."

Anna's shoulders sagged, her stomach tied itself into knots. No! She didn't love her other children more... did she?

"Well, her birth was pretty difficult, very traumatic," said Doc Farnum. "Maybe it would help if you could explain that to her."

"Oh for heaven's sake—I couldn't talk to her about that. She's too young. She'd never understand." Anna's neck grew flushed even thinking of talking about such personal things with her fifteen-year-old daughter.

"I don't really understand the whole thing," Doc said, "but there is a school of thought nowadays that babies are aware of their birth circumstances, and when it's a particularly difficult time, the child's personality can be adversely affected. That might explain her constant rebelliousness since she was little."

Anna pressed her lips together to stop the trembling. She clutched Neil's hand under the table, and he squeezed hers back gently.

"How can we get through to her at this point?" Neil's face was pale and drawn. "She won't even talk to us."

"Give me some more time with her," suggested Walters. "Let me see what I can draw out of her. But there's a limit to what I can do. Maybe I can convince her to talk to a psychiatrist from Miles City. And then, if we keep working on her, we can set up some dialogue between you."

Anna slumped against Neil. Maybe this would be a light at the end of the tunnel. *Am I deserving of her love? Do I have enough strength for her to lean on?*

~~~

Lizzie awoke from a dream that left her feeling anxious and twitchy. She thrashed around in the bed, tried to rip the tubes from her arm, and barely noticed someone enter the room.

"Hey, mellow out, girl. I brought ya somethin'." The voice finally sank into Lizzie's feverish brain, and she looked up to see Hank holding out a hand-rolled joint. "This oughta getcha through the day." He lit it, taking a deep drag himself before passing it to her.

She closed her eyes and took a deep inhale. A calm descended over her immediately. Oh blessed relief. Why couldn't she buy these like regular cigarettes? She sighed, her body oozing back onto the pillows.

"What's this? Who are you?" A booming voice split Lizzie's sense of peace. Doc Farnum. She grimaced. *Busted.*

The doctor grabbed the weed from her with one hand, the other fastened like a pair of vice grips around Hank's arm. "Answer me. Who are you?" He turned to the nurse who had followed him into the room. "Call the sheriff right away," he ordered.

"No!" Lizzie flung her legs over the side of the bed, but the room swayed. The nurse quickly laid her back on the pillows.

"Stay put now," she ordered.

"What's your name?" the doctor asked again through clenched teeth.

The pudgy young man blanched as Doc roughly forced him into a chair. "Hank."

"Hank, what?"

"Hank... Morgan," he said, finally.

"Where you from?"

"Wynona."

~~~

Standing in the hallway just outside Lizzie's hospital room, Anna gasped. Hank Morgan. That crooked banker had a son. A son who brought drugs to her daughter. *Ach, nein.* She sagged against the wall, no longer able to fight the darkness.

CHAPTER FIFTEEN

Anna drew a fortifying breath, picked up the phone and dialed the Wynona Bank. When she heard Morgan's voice, she let out her breath and tried to remain calm. "Mr. Morgan, it's Anna Moser."

"Oh, hello, Mrs. Moser, and how can I be of help today?" His smooth tone grated on her nerves.

"Morgan, I want you to please tell your son to stay away from my daughter Lizzie."

"Really? Your daughter? And why should I do that?"

"Because he's gotten a fifteen-year-old girl into drugs. He should be old enough to know better."

The banker laughed. "He's an adult—I don't tell him what to do any more—you know how that is, I'm sure."

Anna's cheeks fired with heat and she pounded her fist on the desk. "I'm warning you, Morgan. If he comes near Lizzie again, I'll call the sheriff. She *is* underage." She gritted her teeth.

"Now, now, Mrs. Moser, just calm down. After all, he spent several nights in jail because of her. I had to come up with some big money to bail him out. And he could face up to a year, if convicted." His voice lowered. "I'll ask him to curb his appetites. That's all I can do." He hung up.

Anna slammed the phone down. That *Schweinhund...* She gritted her teeth. The one mistake she'd made, asking for a loan when Neil was sick—she'd thought that was in the past, but now it was coming back to haunt her. She allowed a quick smile. *So the little creep went to jail. Good! Just not long enough.*

~~~

The rest of that school year was pure hell. Anna couldn't focus on the ranch or housework. She kept replaying conversations in her head that she'd had with all her children, and trying to rewrite them. Maybe if I'd said this... Maybe if I hadn't said that... Maybe Monica would've stayed closer to home. Maybe Kevin wouldn't have gone away. And maybe Lizzie wouldn't have this sickness, this deep hate and confusion. These thoughts chased her through the days, evolving into a headache. She tossed and turned at night, rising exhausted only to find herself on the merry-go-round again.

She and Neil worked with Coach Walters, then with a psychiatrist from Miles City. Gradually it got so that Lizzie would talk a little with them, then a little more. She stayed in the hospital until she had regained enough weight to satisfy Doc Farnum. But after that, she didn't want to come home.

"I want to go back to school, Mom."

Anna gulped. "Are you sure you're feeling strong enough?"

"Yeah, I'm fine." Lizzie flexed her bicep. "See?"

Anna smiled. "You are looking a lot better. I'm so glad." She gave her a hug, thrilled when Lizzie didn't push her away.

She worried her daughter would get back into her old eating habits, but she promised she wouldn't. And Coach Walters assured her and Neil that between him and Mrs. Dirning, the dorm mother, they would see that she followed a strict regimen. Her health improved with proper nutrition, and she was able to get back into sports, which she loved so much.

The three of them endured an uneasy truce, and life went on.

Kevin drifted around the southwest, then to Seattle, doing odd jobs and calling when he needed money. Anna tried—oh, how she tried—not to worry about him. But her insides felt like they were being gnawed on by a grizzly bear.

On the other hand, Monica, after assuring her when she got engaged that they were not in a hurry to get married, called in May to say she and Tom had set a wedding date—in August.

"Which year?" Anna asked, in shock.

Monica laughed. It was a compromise, she said. She wanted to wait; Tom wanted to get married right away. It would be that coming August.

Instantly the planning began, and in July Anna went to Missoula to help Monica sew her wedding dress. Lizzie was home, helping her dad with haying, and promised to keep him well-fed while her mom was gone. With a deep breath and some trepidation, she left the two alone.

During that visit, she got to know Tom a little better—he pulled her chair out for her at meals, opened the car door for her and Monica, and asked questions about Germany, listening intently. But she was still a little suspicious of this stranger who was stealing away her precious girl. To her, he seemed so different from Neil, carefree with a gift of gab. Would he be able to take care of her daughter? Anna prayed that he would.

~~~

The Saturday morning sun smiled through silken veils of clouds upon the guests gathering for the garden wedding in Missoula. The trees rippled gently in the breeze. The temperature was a perfect seventy-eight degrees. Tom's mother, Dorothy Davis, had outdone herself with her yard. The grass was manicured to green velvet perfection, the roses were in bloom like never before, and the bright gladiolas nodded as though pleased with the upcoming union.

Anna moved among the long tables in her shimmery pink dress, a rare purchase for the occasion. She arranged cheerful petunia-filled bowls from her own garden as centerpieces. Dorothy joined her in directing the caterer placing the three-tiered cake, with its pink climbing roses and waterfall.

"A little more toward the center..."

"Back a smidgen..." It had to be just right.

Anna surveyed the back yard with a smile. Everything was fabulous, down to the strains of Mozart from the tape player being run by a friend of Monica's. Anna felt a gentle tug at her heart. This was Monica's wedding day. Suddenly her palms were wet and her knees began to shake. Why was *she* so nervous? That was supposed to be reserved for the bride.

For a moment, she recalled a wintry, pine-filled church and a bride in a navy blue dress beaming up at a tall, dark-haired, handsome young man. Twenty-six years ago. Where had those years gone? Now it was her first-born's turn.

"Has anybody seen Monica? It's almost ten o'clock." Tom's booming voice interrupted Anna's thoughts. She blinked back a rising tear and smiled at the nervous groom who checked his watch once again as he paced the patio.

"She had an appointment at the beauty shop at eight, but she hasn't come back yet." Anna glanced at Bill, Tom's father. A white-haired, gentle man, he stood to off to one side, a bemused smile tugging at his cheeks.

"Oh, she's chickened out. I just know it." Tom peered around the corner of the house, looking up and down the street. "She probably came to her senses and left town."

Anna couldn't help but laugh. A sense of humor even under stressful conditions. "Well, don't worry. It always takes us women a little longer to get beautiful on our wedding day."

The tires of a maroon Chevy Bel Air squealed as the car shot around the curve and pulled up in front of the Davis house. "There she is," called Jacki, Monica's maid of honor. "Get back in the yard, Tom, you're not supposed to see the bride before the ceremony."

Monica dashed up the sidewalk, her veil trailing from her hand. "Sorry I'm late. It took them ages—much longer than at the practice session." Her long gold ringlets bounced around her head and cascaded down her back as she sprinted up the steps. "I had this image of some cop stopping me for speeding through 'malfunction junction' on a yellow light. But I had my veil ready just in case. Then he would simply have to feel guilty for making me late for my own wedding…"

"And release a pretty girl like you for a ransom," Bill finished.

Everyone laughed, but Anna breathed a small sigh of relief.

Tugging, shushing and giggling, friends Jacki and Sandi rushed Monica into the bedroom to change her into her wedding gown. Lizzie waited with a big welcoming smile, already dressed in her pastel floral bridesmaid dress, and gave Monica a quick hug.

Anna watched in awe as she became enshrouded in a whirl of white satin, lace and pearls. Her attendants gave her a last flick of mascara, a brush of blush, and spritz of hairspray amid flashes from the woman photographer preserving the act of preparation.

"There, you're ready," Sandi announced and stepped back to admire their handiwork. "Gorgeous."

"Just a minute." Anna entered the circle surrounding her daughter, clutching a small blue velvet box. "I want you to have these." She could still picture Neil on one knee that Christmas Eve on their tenth anniversary, shyly presenting her with that blue box, tied with a silver bow.

Monica's eyes widened as she took out the tiny diamond studs. "Oh, Mom, thank you. I've always loved these, and I know how much they mean to you. I'll treasure them always." She stooped to hug her mother, then peered into the mirror to put on the earrings.

"Look, aren't they just beautiful? Okay. Now I'm ready."

Anna's eyes filled as she gazed at her daughter, the bride.

The traditional strains of the "Wedding March" followed Neil and Monica as they walked slowly down the grassy aisle. Tom waited under the maple tree with the minister and Kevin, the best man. He'd arrived the day before from his travels around the country. Anna watched her tall, handsome son with pride. *Thank goodness he's okay.*

As Neil released their daughter's arm and prepared to sit, she stopped, reached up and planted a kiss on his cheek. Then, with a big smile, she turned toward her future husband.

"Isn't she beautiful?" Neil blinked rapidly as he sat down next to Anna, checking his suit pants pocket for a handkerchief. She took his hand and smiled through her own tears.

"Dearly beloved…" The minister held his hand over the couple to bless them. Then he opened his Bible and read:

"Love is patient. Love is kind. Love is not jealous; it does not put on airs, it is not snobbish. Love does nothing rude. It is not self-seeking; it is not prone to anger. It does not brood over injuries, but rejoices with the truth. Love covers over everything, believes everything, hopes for everything, puts up with everything. Love never fails…"

Anna listened as the minister read the familiar passage from Corinthians. Yes, love was wonderful … but would it put food on the table?

~~~

The rest of August flew by in the dust, chaff and straw of harvesting wheat and barley. Kevin and Lizzie were both home and had resumed their close relationship, teasing and joking with each other. Anna smiled often as she cooked and baked, washed and cleaned for her family. If only Monica and Tom lived close by, everything would be perfect.

Anna worried about Kevin's long and unruly hair, with all the "redneck" cowboys around. The people around Horse Creek and Foster didn't take too kindly to "long-haired hippies." She remembered with a sinking heart when one of Monica's classmates had come home from college for the summer a couple of years ago. He had gone into Foster one Saturday night, had been caught in the street by a group of drunken cowboys, thrown to the ground and held there while they hacked off his long hair with their pocket knives.

She had tried to talk to Kevin about getting it cut, but was met with stony silence. She had been so happy and relieved to see him at Monica's wedding.

"So, you've had quite the year traveling around the country." She tried to fish for more information.

"Yup." He smiled and shrugged.

"What was Houston like?"

"Hot. Humid."

"Did you like Seattle better?"

He shrugged again. "Some. Pretty rainy."

Anna sighed and finally gave up. Perhaps not knowing spared her some worries. In time, she hoped he would have the courage to open that door.

Lizzie seemed eager to get out into the fields and help her dad and brother. She had regained her old energy, along with a healthy weight, and showed a new attitude toward life. She even started to come to church with the family again, and sat around the table after supper, talking and laughing with them. *Such a relief.*

One day, after driving a truckload of wheat in from the field, she bounced into the kitchen at noontime. "Hi, Mom! Mmm, something sure smells good." She peeked into the pots on the stove. "By the way, thanks for all the cooking you do. You sure take good care of us." She turned back toward Anna and paused. "I love you, Mom."

Warmth radiated through Anna's chest. She threw her arms out wide. She had so rarely heard those words from her youngest daughter. Oh, thank you, Lord, she prayed silently as she hugged Lizzie. Her daughter squeezed back for a moment before she took off again.

But the idyllic season passed all too quickly. In September, Lizzie returned to Foster High for her junior year, and Kevin decided to go back to Missoula to study auto mechanics.

On a frosty November evening, Anna and Neil settled in the living room after supper. She inserted a burned-out light bulb into one of Neil's wool socks and began the laborious process of mending the heel. First she stitched several rows of long threads across the hole, then started perpendicular rows, over one thread, under the next, weaving a new heel. She settled into a rhythm as her husband sprawled on the couch, half-dozing.

The phone rang, startling them. "Probably Monica. She hasn't called in a while." Anna set down her darning and walked to the desk to answer.

"*Liebe Anna, Karl hier.*"

A phone call from Germany. *Ach du lieber.* Adrenaline shot through Anna's body. "What's wrong?—*Was ist los?*"

Her brother's voice broke. "*Mutti ... Sie ist heute gestorben...*"

Mutti? Dead? "*Ach, Gott im Himmel.*" Anna's hand shook as she crossed herself, the old Catholic ways coming back automatically.

It was their mother's heart, Karl told her. She had been on medication for years, felt a little more tired lately, and suddenly... she was gone. The funeral service would be in three days... no need for Anna to come...

She half-fell into the chair. Neil jumped up from the couch, knelt beside her and held her shaking hand while she finished the phone conversation, then gathered her in his arms as the sobs came. "Oh, *Mutti, meine Mutti!*"

During the next few weeks Anna wandered aimlessly in a fog. She worked through the chores outside and the cleaning and cooking inside as though she were a robot. She thought of the way Mutti had been when she was growing up—always working, in the fields, in the house; cleaning, keeping their little house spotless, and finding something for them to eat, even when food was scarce. Mutti had given up a lot for her children, even trading off her heirloom jewelry after the war so they could eat.

Anna pictured her mother before the war years in the tiny, but cozy kitchen. As a little girl she cherished the tantalizing smell of baking bread, the sharp aroma of cooking sausages, the simmering hearty soups. And once again, Anna could feel the warm, yeast-and-cinnamon hugs—oh, those hugs, how she missed them. How she had missed her mother all these years. Now there would be no chance to regain what she'd given up by coming to America.

Her days were silent. The kids weren't around anymore, Neil worked in the fields or in the shop all day. She threw herself into attacking weeds in the garden, scrubbing floors until the finish threatened to evaporate, driving tractor when Neil needed help, and sewing for the girls.

"I don't know why I bother," she told Neil. "I'm sure they never wear anything I make anyway." But she couldn't stop. It was a link to her daughters, a thread that surely would be severed if she quit doing things for them.

After Lizzie's problems, the neighbor women finally stopped calling to fish for gossip. Anna had heard the terrible things that were said—Lizzie was in the hospital for a drug overdose, Lizzie was a drug dealer. Anna couldn't bring herself to go to the Horse Creek store for weeks after that. She couldn't bear to show her face, wondering what they were saying about her now.

And her own children—not a word of sympathy from them, not a card, not even a phone call after Neil had called to tell them about their Oma. They were all immersed in their own worlds. They didn't understand the pain.

Aloneness seeped into her soul like the cold winter winds. It hurt so deeply. All these years being estranged from her mother, she'd vowed not to make the same mistakes with her children. A lightning bolt thought struck her—*But I have. I'm not close to my own children*. Something had pushed a wedge into each relationship somewhere along the line. And time only seemed to deepen the gap.

The seasons came and went. Anna felt numb to the cold, indifferent to the heat. She began to understand on a much deeper level why Neil had become so withdrawn after his parents died, why he had been so depressed. At the time she wished he would talk more about his feelings and try to rise above his sadness. *Here I am, doing the same thing.*

Now Neil treated her with quiet tenderness, coming in mid-afternoon to make coffee and serve her cookies he'd picked up at the store. He held her hand or put an arm around her more often. "It's okay to feel sad," he said when the tears came once again.

She smiled at him through her grief. *Dear Neil. He understands. He is my rock.*

Even though it had been twenty-six years since she'd left home, Anna felt the void as though they'd been together every day. And Mutti had been there—in her thoughts. Anna was always writing a letter in her head, wondering how Mutti did things, how she coped with raising children, how she dealt with growing older. She would never again see her mother. A part of Anna had died.

CHAPTER SIXTEEN

One bright spring morning, Anna eagerly ripped open the letter from Monica. What a rare treat to hear from her daughter nowadays.

> *...Kevin moved out a few weeks ago, said he was getting an apartment with a friend from school. He's doing OK, as far as I can tell. Seems to like Vo-Tech and mechanics. Probably good for him. I met his girlfriend the other day—Lisa. She's a cute little girl, very friendly, outgoing. I like her.*

Oh dear. Anna lowered the letter to her lap and gazed out the living room window. A moth beat its wings against the screen. An apartment with a "friend." That probably meant Kevin was living with his girlfriend. Her little Kevy. The empty spot in her heart turned cavernous.

She sighed deeply, shaking her head. She couldn't take care of him any longer. Had she held on to her children too tightly? Her son was beyond her grasp, like the terrible dream she still had so often.

~~~

Lizzie pushed her books away and put her head on her desk in the cramped dorm room. She couldn't take it anymore—being good, studying hard, making good grades. The pressure accelerated through her senior year. To qualify for a sports scholarship to college, she not only had to excel in all the sports, but also keep her grades up, fill out applications, eat what she was told to, and do what everybody expected of her.

A roaring sound built in her ears. "Eat this. Don't smoke marijuana anymore. Study. Stay in. Don't go out." The familiar pain began at the base of her neck, rising like hot mercury up over her crown, down behind her eyes. Lizzie pounded her fist on the desk and tears oozed from her clenched eyelids. How much longer could she keep up this charade, making her mom and dad and Coach Watson think she was all better? Normal now. Normal? She'd never been normal. Never would be. Didn't want to be, if it meant giving in to all this pressure, never having any fun. She'd be better off dead.

A rattle at the window startled her. She opened her eyes and raised her head. The light hurt her eyes. The rattle came again. Someone was throwing pebbles at her second-floor dorm window. Lizzie grimaced in pain as she raised the sash and peered down.

"Hank. Long time, no see."

"Hey, Lizzie, come on down. It's a gorgeous day. Wanna take a ride to Miles City?"

Suddenly the pain in her head began to subside. Yes, that was it. Just forget about homework for one afternoon. Go on a joyride.

"Be right down." She grabbed a sweatshirt, swiped a brush in the general direction of her hair and ran down the stairs to where Hank waited in his red Mustang convertible.

"Oooh. You're my knight in shining armor today. Just couldn't take another minute of staring at those books." Lizzie cracked the beer he tossed her as he peeled out of the graveled parking lot.

Hank grinned. "Then you could probably use a little distraction." He reached into his pocket and held out a familiar-looking pill. Lizzie broke into a smile. Acid. She remembered that dreamy, colorful trip, and how she'd felt so happy, so peaceful.

"Far out. You know exactly what a girl needs." She washed the pill down with the beer and leaned back into the seat. The warm spring sun soaked her face, while the freedom of the wind blew through her hair. She could breathe again.

~~~

Anna studied the woman at the end of the aisle and pretended to read the label on the can before putting it into her shopping cart. Wasn't that...? Yes, it was Velma Green. Her husband owned that big ranch a few miles down the road where Evelyn and Larry worked. Would she say hello?

The woman came toward her, pushing her cart and gazing intently at the shelves. Anna held up her list, peering at Velma out of the corner of her slitted eyes. The woman reached for something high on the shelf. She wasn't going to notice Anna. Shyness enveloped her like a shroud. Her hands were sweaty. Should she say something?

Then Velma turned toward her. "Oh, hello there. Didn't see you. So intent on my list, I have tunnel vision." She chuckled.

Anna took a deep breath and smiled. "Hello, Velma. How are you today?"

The neighbor woman exchanged pleasantries about the weather and cattle for a minute, and then her face turned serious. "Did you hear that Emily Mitchell's mother died last week? It must be so hard for her."

Anna blinked. "Um... no, I didn't." She tightened clammy hands around the cart handle. *My Mutti just died. Doesn't she realize I must be sad too?* Then she shook her head to clear it. *Well, of course not. I guess I didn't tell anyone around here.* "I'm really sorry to hear that. Yes, it is very sad to lose your mother—I know about that. Thank you for telling me."

They parted, and Anna gathered more baking supplies. When she got home she spent the afternoon preparing a roast and potatoes and baked a cake. She packed everything into a box and at the last minute added a plastic bag of cookies out of the freezer.

As she drove the fifteen miles to the Mitchell ranch, she found herself clenching the wheel with clammy fingers. Moths leapt and cavorted in her middle. *Am I doing the right thing?* Emily Mitchell had never been the least bit friendly or warm toward

Anna, and her kids had bullied Monica and Kevin unmercifully when they were younger.

She swallowed a sharp bit of bile. *This is what neighbors do here in Montana. We help each other out in times of need.* Driving up to the front of the house, she took a deep breath, grabbed the box of food and marched onto the porch.

After several minutes, Mrs. Mitchell opened the door, holding a fussing toddler. Her eyes widened and she swiped at the stringy tendrils of hair hanging in her face.

"Hello, Emily. I'm really sorry to hear about your mother." She looked down at the box in her arms. "I... uh... brought some food."

"Oh. Yes. Thank... thank you." The woman darted a glance behind her and then opened the door wider. "Um... come in." She sighed. "Sorry about the mess. Non-stop company, and my daughter, well, she's in town looking for a job, so... she left the kids with me." As if on cue the toddler let out a squall and Emily bounced her on her hip.

Anna swept aside a mound of unfolded laundry on the table and set the box down. She took out the bag of cookies and offered one to the child who grew quiet. "May I make you a cup of coffee, Emily?"

Mrs. Mitchell sighed. "Yes. That would be very nice, thank you."

When the coffee was ready, Anna poured them both a cup, set the cookies on a plate, and sat. "I just wanted to tell you, my mother passed away a few weeks ago too, so I know what you must be going through."

Her neighbor's brows arched. "She did? I didn't know. In Germany?"

Anna nodded. "Yes. And of course, I wasn't able to go back for her funeral. It's been six years since I visited my family there."

Emily's gray eyes moistened. "That must be hard. My mother lived with us the last few years and was very sick this past year." She looked up as noisy footsteps clattered down the stairs.

Two boys, around six or seven, chased each other through the living room and into the kitchen, whooping and yelling. "And my daughter's husband... well, they're separated, and she and her kids are here now." Her shoulders slumped.

"Cookies! Can we have a cookie?" one of the boys yelled.

Anna stood. "Yes, you may, if you'll sit very quietly with a glass of milk and give your grandma a moment of peace, okay?"

They nodded and sat at the table. Anna poured them the milk and gave them each a cookie. Then she looked at Mrs. Mitchell. "Now, do you mind if I help you fold these clothes?"

~~~

Lizzie grinned and screamed into the wind. "Faster! Faster!" The powerful engine howled as the speedometer climbed. The red car clung to the winding road, soaring through the straight stretches, screeching around curves.

First the velvety green of newly planted fields flashed by, then an occasional farmer working the soil on his tractor. They zoomed past the lone cottonwood tree where a fake sign shaped like an official forest service seal read, "Rock Springs National Forest."

Laughter bubbled up inside Lizzie. The tension that had been building for so long released at last. She laughed at everything Hank said, at the farmers in the fields, at the mock forest sign. She alternately doubled over, then rocked back against the seat, flinging her arms out behind her, shrieking with uncontrollable laughter.

She couldn't stop. Hysteria took over her body. The fields became a rushing blur, the highway a dark ribbon reaching for the sky. Now she was in a rocket ship, hurtling through space, objects flying straight at her.

The crazed laughter came from somewhere outside her, a diabolical sound that turned her blood to ice. It chased her faster and faster through the darkening universe.

She screamed. "Stop! Stop it! Oh, help me!" Her arms flailed out at the thing that was attacking her, now grabbing hold of the wheel.

He recoiled from her blows, struggling to hold onto the steering wheel. Lizzie's arms and fists were everywhere, in his face, hitting his chest, his head. She howled like the demons that played with her brain, her face hot and contorted. The speedometer read one hundred ten. Lizzie grabbed the wheel. The demon, now with Hank's face, pulled back. The car swerved, corrected, swerved again. The tires screeched, smoked on the asphalt. Gravel sprayed up from the shoulder of the road.

As they struggled, a loud air horn rent the air. She looked up to see the huge silver radiator of the Peterbilt looming directly in front of them.

~~~

The dim light faded in the narrow tunnel. Anna could hear them talking—Monica and Kevin and Neil and a bunch of other people. Her little family, all together again. Yet, something was missing. What was it? She strained to remember. She could see them all, gathered around the mound of fresh earth. But she was looking through the wrong end of a telescope. The crowd was so far away, their quiet murmurs a mere buzzing in the wind. Someone hugged her. Said something. She stood like a statue, frozen in time, looking down that narrow tube.

Anna allowed herself to be led back to the car. She sat, a cold block of ice, between the warm bodies of her husband and daughter. Monica sniffled and held a tissue to her eyes. Neil said something to Kevin in the front seat. The car hummed and swayed, but she couldn't hear. Couldn't feel.

At the house, Neil opened the car door and got out, reaching a hand back to help her. His long arms wrapped around her, and she allowed him to lead her inside. In the kitchen were more people, dishing up heaping plates from steaming casseroles on the table. The reverse telescope distorted their tear-stained faces as they muttered toward her. Anna felt her way along the sides of the tunnel, through the kitchen, into the living room, through the hallway and into the blessed darkness of the bedroom. She lay down and pulled the covers over her head.

CHAPTER SEVENTEEN

Neil stood in the darkened room and watched his wife wrestling beneath the covers. Her face twitched, and she shook her head violently from side to side. She moaned. "No. No."

He smoothed his hand over her forehead. "It's okay, honey. I'm here."

She exhaled a deep sigh, turned onto her side and breathed deeply again.

He stayed near the bed, looking at her for a long time. With a sigh, he plodded out to the kitchen to fry some eggs for his supper. He sat alone, looking at the scrambled mess on his plate. He took a bite, but could not swallow past the lump in his throat. He put down his fork and cradled his head in his hands. And then the sobs came, convulsing his body.

"What am I going to do?" he cried aloud into the emptiness. The unanswerable call of the bereaved echoed in his head. His profound sense of loss was palpable, a living entity in itself. Their Lizzie was gone. It wasn't supposed to happen that way. Parents weren't supposed to bury their children.

And now, his wife seemed lost to him, too.

Throughout the past winter, she had already settled into quiet grieving over her mother. Her usual spark had dimmed, her enthusiasm for ranch work greatly subdued. Neil understood, remembering how he had felt when his parents died. He had stood back through the loss of Anna's mother, quiet and patient, letting her have her time to heal, hoping she would gradually return to their normal, everyday life.

But since Lizzie's death... Anna had barely spoken ten words. She often lay in the darkened bedroom during the day, and prowled the house, sleepless, at night. She wouldn't talk to Monica or Kevin when they called. She wouldn't come out when

143

a neighbor stopped by. He had no idea how to cope with this stranger, his wife. Anna had always been the one who talked things through, who came up with ideas and solutions, who kept him on track. Neil sat in the helpless silence. The scrambled eggs in front of him looked much like the chaos his life had become. With a tightness in his chest he rose, wondering what more the future had in store for them.

~~~

Kevin stood over the VW, sleepless nights weighing heavy on his shoulders since he'd been back to Missoula after the funeral.

"Ready?" His fellow students at Vo-Tech prepared to lift the engine out of the bug.

Kevin nodded. As he grabbed hold, his back suddenly froze in agonizing pain.

He went to his apartment to spend a week lying on the couch, alternately sleeping and moaning. Lisa stayed close by, bringing him aspirin, water and food.

He didn't want to think about his sister, and as long as he was asleep he didn't have to. But when he awoke, the memories of his laughing, teasing, little sis tried to sneak in between the spasms of excruciating pain in his back. He gave in to the pain, welcoming it, letting it take over his mind.

~~~

Monica walked through her life in a daze. She went to work each day at the newspaper, but often found herself sitting at her desk, staring off into space. She couldn't bring herself to pick up the phone, to make appointments, to write the articles she needed to write.

Her sister was dead. How could this be possible? Things like this didn't happen in little, isolated Foster, Montana. She'd never even *heard* of acid or marijuana when she was in high school. As a journalist, she searched for answers. *I should have been there more for her, let her share her feelings with me.* Guilt gnawed at her insides.

She shook her head. But for heaven's sake, they were ten years apart—she was hardly ever around when Lizzie was growing up. Monica could argue logic with herself, but somehow she still felt she was to blame.

She put her head in her hands. They had never really gotten along. Why couldn't she have been the kind of person to draw Lizzie out? She'd obviously needed help. Monica had known that when she noticed her sister's eating problems. But no, it was easier, safer, to stay here in her own life, four hundred miles away, and not think of her family back on the ranch.

At home, with Tom, Monica put on a brave face. "Everything is fine. Life goes on." Secretly she wrapped up the idea of Lizzie's death into a neat little package, tied it up with string, and put it on a shelf in the back of her mind, along with the fact-packages of Abraham Lincoln's death, the death of her grandparents, and other details of life. And then she shut the door and locked it.

~~~

The light in the tunnel was still dim for Anna. At first, she had trouble focusing on day-to-day life. She could only cope by sleeping the days away. And at night, when she couldn't sleep anymore, she sat, numb, staring out at the moonlit prairie, grasses waving silver in the night breeze. Then restlessness overcame her, and she paced from room to room. She stopped in Lizzie's bedroom to smooth the bedspread, hang up a discarded blouse, or retrieve a tennis shoe from under the bed. She would not—could not—allow herself to face the truth. Her daughter was only away at school for the week.

Like the body shutting down the pain receptors after a physical trauma, Anna's mind also shut down. There was no pain, only numbness. Neil gazed at her silently from the mouth of her tunnel, questions in his wounded eyes. But she had no answers.

She couldn't be there for him. It was as though she, herself, no longer existed.

Neil woke her one evening. "Bad news." He put his hand on her shoulder. "The sheriff just called. They're not going to charge Hank in the accident."

"What?" Anna sat up on the edge of the bed.

Neil shook his head. "The truck driver testified he saw Lizzie wrestling with the wheel right before the car hit. The coroner's jury concluded Hank was not at fault."

"Not at fault?" Her voice screeched. "He gave her drugs, and he's not at fault?" She clenched her hands into fists and pounded Neil's chest. "*Ach Gott. Ach Gott.* He killed her. He killed her."

Neil captured her hands in his, pulled her to him and stilled her with soft murmurs. "I know, *Liebchen*, I know."

With gulping, guttural sobs, she sank back and slid beneath the covers. If only she would go to sleep and never wake up.

Late that night, long after Neil had fallen asleep, Anna paced the house. The gray fog that had occupied her tunnel for the past several weeks changed to a furious red mist that swirled and undulated before her eyes. Rage replaced numbness. Pain pierced her heart.

An intense volcano of hate and anger rose from some inner core. Her eyes were open wide, her mind sharp with acute pain. Jeremy Morgan. That, that lying, cheating, slimy snake… and his murderous son. Anna balled her fists so tight her arms shook. Every time she passed the phone desk, she paused. She had an uncontrollable urge to wake Morgan, to scream at him, call him every horrible name she'd ever heard—in German and in English.

Picking up the receiver, she put it down again. She drummed her fingernails on the desk, walked into the kitchen, but turned abruptly back to the phone. This time she dialed.

Morgan answered, his voice thick with sleep. "Do you know what time it is?"

"Of course I know what time it is, you *Schweinhund*." She heard his sharp intake of breath. "My daughter is dead. Your despicable son lives and gets off scot-free."

"But he's—"

Anna wouldn't let him speak. "You knew he was dealing drugs. How could you let him do this? I hate you! Hate you both!" Anna slammed the receiver so hard the phone bell clanged in protest. She pounded her fist on the desk and wailed. "*Ach Gott, lieber Gott im Himmel.* Why have you forsaken me?"

Neil bolted into the room with wide eyes, knelt beside her and gently cradled her as she cried, at long last. "I'm so mad. I hate him so. Why did this have to happen? Just when she was doing so much better. Why? Why? Why?"

Neil rocked her, patting her back and smoothing her hair. "I know. I know," he whispered, then his voice changed to a raspy growl. "We'll get him. That devil will have to pay."

They sat like that, in the cold silence of the night—the tears flowing, their thoughts confused—clinging to each other. "Thank God we have each other." Neil's pain flowed out with his words, comforting her.

"It's all we have left." Anna wrenched the words from her core.

She'd thought calling him in the middle of the night would be more satisfying, would ease her pain.

But it wasn't enough. Not enough to wake Morgan at 2 a.m. and scream obscenities at him. She wanted to meet up with him in a dark alley and pound her fists into his face until its vision was erased from her memory forever.

Her mind flashed to Neil's 30.06 propped in the closet. She could almost feel her hands close around the smooth wood stock and the long, cold barrel as she sighted the rifle on the middle of Morgan's forehead. She felt her finger on the hard steel of the trigger, slowly tightening, beginning the process of sending cold death down the long black barrel. Or maybe the pistol, smaller, easier to handle—

No! That would be too easy, too quick. He needed to suffer as much as she was. Anna shook her head like a wet dog. No! *This is wrong, I know it. It's no longer an "eye for an eye."*

~~~

The next day, Neil came into the house, mumbling something about the solenoid on the tractor. After making several phone calls, he stepped into the kitchen, where Anna sat, swirling the black dregs in her coffee cup. "I need a part for the John Deere, and the only place that has one is the dealer in Wynona. Do you feel like running in to pick it up for me?"

At first, she cringed inside. The thought of driving somewhere by herself, facing people, made her nauseated. She stared at the inky mess in the bottom of her cup. Morgan's face seemed to leer at her from the slime. Anna looked up at Neil. "Sure. I'll go. I don't have anything better to do." She smiled. "It'll do me good to get out of the house."

She dressed carefully in a wine-colored polyester pantsuit, brushed waves into her hair and even applied lipstick. Then she drove the fifty miles to Wynona with a cold, steady eye on the road, not allowing herself to think, not even registering the summer colors of the prairie. In town, the car seemed to steer itself to a parking spot right in front of the bank's front door. Anna picked up her black patent leather purse and marched inside.

"May I help you?" The secretary outside Morgan's office stood up, ineffectually waving her arm as Anna swept past, twisted the knob, and barged in.

Jeremy Morgan jerked back in his chair. She slammed the door, planted her palms on top of his desk and leaned forward, nearly in his face. "Why have you done this to me?"

The banker's face colored. "I haven't done anything to you. It was an accident, and your daughter was at fault."

"Your slimy son gave her drugs—that's what caused it. I've lost my child, and you ..." Anna's words hissed from between clenched teeth, "you still have everything."

"Hank is still in the hospital, in a full body cast! What on earth do you want from me?"

She pounded her purse on the desk. "Perhaps your customers would like to know how you took advantage of a woman in need, giving her a loan, and then trying to foreclose."

He snorted. "Ha. That is an unfounded accusation, and you know it." He narrowed his eyes. "I could tell the sheriff about your 2 a.m. phone call, harassing me, a fine, upstanding citizen."

Anna straightened. "We'll just see about that." A wave of dizziness washed over her. "I hope you *and* your son rot in hell."

Morgan's smile leered at her, became disembodied, lingered in the air as blackness closed around her.

Anna opened her eyes to see a woman bathing her face with cold water. "Are you all right?" she asked.

"What happened? Where am I?" Then she remembered. Morgan's office. Morgan's secretary.

The woman helped Anna to her feet and to a chair. "I'll get you some water."

Ice filled her veins. She stood, faced Morgan, and forced the words to come. "I never want to see you—or your devil spawn—again. There's nothing more you can do to me." She reached forward and swept papers, pens, and a coffee cup off the desk with a resounding crash. She turned and walked out of his office, one foot in front of the other, her head high, shoulders straight.

In the car, she put it in gear, backed out of the parking spot and pointed the Buick down the highway, numbness again overtaking her.

Somehow she made it home. Anna had no recollection of the trip. Her life was over. Her daughter was gone, dead because of the Morgans. And he'd tell everybody about her calls, her visit. A nice ripe, juicy piece of gossip this would be in the neighborhood. *That German woman. We always knew she was a little off.*

Neil met her at the door. "Hi, Hon. I have coffee on. Did you get the part all right?"

Anna stopped and stared at him. The part. For the tractor. That's what she'd gone to town for. She began to laugh hysterically.

Neil frowned and looked at her quizzically. "What's the matter? What's so funny?"

"I-I for-forgot the part." Her knees jellied.

"What?" Neil frowned and stepped to her side.

She sat heavily in a kitchen chair. "I went to see Morgan, but he laughed at me. Oh, Neil, I only wanted him to acknowledge what his son did, wanted an apology, a kind word." She erupted into sobs.

Neil cradled her, and they sat rocking together, their tears mingling.

~~~

About a week later, Anna answered the phone to hear an unfamiliar woman's voice. "Mrs. Moser, this is Sylvia from the Wynona Bank, Mr. Morgan's secretary."

Anna's stomach lurched. No doubt calling to fuel the gossip chain.

The woman continued. "I wanted to see if you're doing all right. I was concerned about you fainting the other day."

Her mind did a double-take. "Oh … that. No, I'm fine. Just didn't have much to eat, I guess."

"Well …" Sylvia hesitated. "This is probably none of my business, but …"

Anna bit her lip. *Here it comes—the whole world will know about my visit.*

"…Did Mr. Morgan ever have dealings with you and your husband that caused financial problems?"

She couldn't believe her ears. What was this woman trying to say? "Ah… I…"

"No, no. It's okay," Sylvia spoke quickly. "There's something strange going on around here, some citizens' group talking about suing over foreclosures. It's all very hush-hush. I'm sorry. I shouldn't have mentioned it. But I'm glad to know you're feeling better." The secretary said a cordial good-bye and hung up.

Anna's thoughts reeled. So, maybe Jeremy Morgan's bank dealings were not on the up and up after all. Yes, she remembered the neighbor whose brother had lost his place because of Morgan's foreclosure. But it was legal to do that, if someone couldn't make the payments. *Wonder what's going on...?*

An overwhelming urge to connect to Lizzie engulfed Anna, and she stumbled into her daughter's room. One of these days she needed to clean it all out, but she couldn't yet. It would be like erasing Lizzie—and she didn't want to forget her youngest. Idly, she picked up a bag of personal belongings from her dorm room. She hadn't even been able to bring herself to go through these things.

She smoothed and folded the flowered pajamas she'd made, a blouse, a sweater and stacked them on the bed. When she picked up a hooded zip sweatshirt, she felt a lump in the pocket. Anna reached in and took out a prescription bottle. With a frown, she read the label: "Isobel Morgan, Valium..." One pill remained, and it didn't look like any Valium she'd ever seen.

With a sinking heart, Anna went to the phone and dialed the sheriff's office.

~~~

Anna stood at the garden gate, staring at the patch of weeds. It was June, but she had none of her usual desire to let the warm soil sift through her fingers, to count her packets of seeds or to sketch out the rows and hills where everything should grow.

The warmth of the sun beat against her back, but she hardly noticed. She was empty, numb. What was the use? Hoeing weeds that never quit growing, nurturing seedlings that would die from lack of rain—never-ending work. Even if there were vegetables for canning and freezing, who would eat them anyway?

Gradually she became aware of the steady washing-machine beat of an engine. She looked toward the county road, seeing a swirl of dust rising behind a blue Volkswagen bus. It slowed and turned down the half-mile driveway, clattering across the cattle guard onto the Moser property.

Oh, no. Company. Anna plodded back to the house. No, she didn't want company. Couldn't stand to smile and nod and carry on a conversation as if nothing in the world were wrong. She went into her bedroom and closed the door.

After a while she heard voices in the kitchen and the bump and clang of Neil making coffee. She heard a woman's high-pitched voice and a low, quiet, male rumble that seemed somehow familiar. She strained to listen, but couldn't quite make out the words or identify the visitors. Anna went to the door, stood, and listened. Opening it a crack to peek out, Anna was startled by Neil reaching for the doorknob at the same time.

"Oh good, you're awake." He smiled at her. "I think you might want to come join us—Kevin is here."

Anna's heart gave a leap. "Kevin? Is here?" Her eyes filled with moisture. She surged forward to the kitchen door. "Kevy-ah-Kevin…" She stopped short as he rose, tall and bushy-haired. Beside him was a young woman, with flowing sandy hair, dressed in the full, long skirt and hiking boots of the Missoula college crowd.

Kevin kept coming, smiling, his arms out. He half-lifted her in a big bear hug. "Hi, Mom." Letting her regain her feet, he swept an arm toward the girl at the table. "I'd like you to meet Lisa. We're getting married this summer."

Her head swam. It was too much to absorb. She hadn't seen him in months, hadn't even heard from him. *Now, he's here. He's back.* A warmth filled her chest as she looked up at her tall, slender son, and her arms ached to hold the little boy he had been. *He's so thin.* She'd have to feed him. Let's see, what could she cook…? But wait, he'd brought a stranger with him. She blinked. What is this? Who is this? They're getting married? No, no, he's too young for marriage. He still needed his mother. He still needed *her* to take care of him.

Woozy, she stumbled forward and sank into a chair. The girl's earnest face finally wavered into focus, and Anna remembered her manners. "Sorry. I got a little dizzy for a second." She reached out to shake hands. "Nice to meet you, Lisa." She was rewarded with a wide, warm smile and a firm clasp of a hand.

"I'm so excited to finally meet you, Mrs. Moser."

Neil poured coffee and set a plate of store-bought cookies on the table. "So glad you're here." He put a hand on Kevin's shoulder.

Anna's face flushed. Store-bought cookies. She hadn't a thing baked. What must this girl think of her?

"So, how was auto mechanics school?" Neil asked.

"Fine." Kevin bit into a cookie. "Finished up Friday, and we thought we'd head out here right away."

"Didn't you have a graduation ceremony?" Anna looked at her son.

"Yeah, there was one, but I didn't wanna go."

Sadness washed over her. She would have loved to watch her son graduate.

"And are you in school, too?" She studied the girl's huge brown eyes. Just like Kevin's.

"No. Not yet. I've been managing the Vo-Tech bookstore. That's how Kevin and I met."

"I see." Anna sipped her coffee. "You must be from Missoula then…?"

"No, my parents live near Great Falls, but my sister is in Missoula." Lisa grinned at Kevin, who reached out and took her hand.

Neil, Kevin, and Lisa continued their conversation, occasionally making a joke and laughing.

Anna sat quietly. How could other people go on with their lives, as if nothing had happened? How could they laugh? Her only son was thinking of getting married, of leaving her. She put her hand tentatively on his arm. "You'll stay this summer, won't you?"

Kevin and Lisa exchanged looks. "Yeah, uh, that's what we wanted to talk to you about." Kevin hesitated. "Uh...we were wondering if we could come work for you and live here after we get married," he blurted.

Anna's head jerked back in surprise and her heart raced. She looked into Neil's astonished face. They never, in their wildest dreams, had dared to hope Kevin would want to work the place. She tried to blink away her tears.

"I..." Neil's voice turned gravelly, and he stopped to clear his throat. "That would mean more to your mom and me than anything in the world."

Kevin's shoulders relaxed as if a weight had been released suddenly. He leaned back, reaching for Lisa's hand to squeeze it gently. "Well, looks like you're stuck with us then."

That jolted Anna out of her stupor. "Yes!" She jumped up and hugged her son. "Yes. I'm so happy. This is wonderful news." Going to the refrigerator, she grabbed a bottle of white wine. "This calls for a celebration." She took out meat and cheese and filled plates and glasses.

That night as Anna crawled into bed beside Neil, her heart stirred for the first time since Lizzie's death. She reached for his hand. "I'm so glad Kevin is home."

Neil smiled. "Yeah, me too. And Lisa sure seems like a nice girl. I like her."

"Well...we'll have to see... He seems happy." She nestled under the covers. She'd reserve judgment until she got to know Lisa better.

~~~

Anna riffled through the mail, stopped, and peered at the typed envelope without a return address. *Who could that be from?*

Curious, she ripped it open. A newspaper clipping fell out. Her jaw dropped as she saw the headline: BANKER ARRESTED IN DRUG RAID.

"Neil!" Her voice came out as a squawk. "Neil, come quick!"

He ran into the kitchen, a worried frown creasing his brow. "What is it?"

Anna handed him the article with shaking fingers. "You'll never believe this."

The story told of a federal "sting" that had netted several drug dealers in the state, Jeremy and Hank Morgan among them.

Neil lowered the clipping. "That pill bottle you turned over to the sheriff must have helped. I wonder how many other young kids had their lives ruined… " A shadow of the old pain crossed his lined face, and he shook his head sadly.

Anna blinked and swallowed, then put her hand on his arm. "But now they've been caught, and we'll see justice done. I'm so relieved." She took a deep breath, relaxing her shoulders. Finally, vindication. Warmth spread through her body and a buoyancy rose in her chest.

Leaning forward, she kissed his cheek. "Oh, I'm so glad Kevin and Lisa are here. We've got to tell them the good news."

~~~

"Well, this is about the latest I've ever planted a garden, but what the heck, let's give it a try, huh? The soil is still nice and moist." Anna set the paper sack of seed packets on the ground and handed Lisa a stick and the end of a long piece of twine. "Here, put this in the ground right there, will you? I'll go down to the other end, and that way we'll get a nice, straight row."

"That's a good way to do it." Lisa took the string and stretched it tight at the far end of the garden.

Picking up a hoe, Anna dragged it along the line, creating a long, straight furrow. "Now, you can put these pea seeds in; one and a half inches apart, covering them with a half inch of soil."

Although she had them memorized, she read the packet directions out loud one more time for Lisa.

The cloud Anna had dwelt in for so long had lifted. The sun was warmer, and the sky was bluer. Lisa was such a nice girl, so warm and friendly, and so eager to learn. And Anna could think of so much she wanted to teach her.

Together they planted and tended the garden; Lisa learned how to bake bread and how to sew; they embroidered pillowcases, made silk flower bouquets and planned the wedding endlessly.

Kevin and Neil grinned at each other whenever they came in from the hayfields, seeing the two women bustling about the kitchen and talking a mile a minute.

"I'm so glad your mom is feeling better," Neil confided to Kevin. "I was at the end of my rope. That's how much I was worried about her."

"Yeah, looks like they've hit it off. That's a big relief."

But to Kevin in private, Lisa lamented, "I'm trying so hard to fit in here, but, man, your mom is so finicky. The rows have to be perfectly straight in the garden, the kitchen has to be kept just so, if I don't sew a seam just right, I have to rip it out. I don't know if I can do this."

~~~

Neil subscribed to the Billings Gazette where the Morgan trial was being held, and over the next several weeks, the story came out.

"Remember when the neighbors kept having calves disappear?" Anna looked up from the latest article at Neil and Kevin. "It's unbelievable. Morgan was blackmailing ranchers who were having trouble keeping up with their mortgages through his bank."

"Blackmail? You're kidding." Kevin reached for the paper.

"You're right, and that's not all. Listen to this—he told them if they would rustle cattle for him, they could keep their ranches. Some were desperate enough to do that. And, if they threatened to turn him in, he could just implicate them in the rustling. Then he sold the calves for a nice fat profit."

Anna shook her head, incredulous. "Remember George Roberts? Apparently he refused to have anything to do with it, and Morgan foreclosed on his ranch."

"Well, I'll be darned," Neil's eyes widened behind his glasses as he took the article to read for himself.

The story grew more and more bizarre as the trial progressed.

Each day Anna relayed the latest information to Kevin and Lisa. "Sometime in the early '70s he apparently discovered the drug market, and that's where he really made his profit. He even used his own son to build that market with his age group. Hank made friends with kids like Lizzie and got 'em hooked." Her neck heated as she remembered. "And *he* got to live." She closed her eyes, took in a deep breath and exhaled slowly. "Sorry. It still makes me see red when I think about it."

Lisa put her arm around her future mother-in-law's shoulder and squeezed gently. "I know. I wish I would've known Lizzie. Maybe I could have helped, somehow…"

"No, honey, none of us could. It's in the past, and I have finally forgiven the Morgans' rottenness. They will receive their just reward."

The next set of headlines read:
"MORGANS SENTENCED"
"Montana Drug Kings' Reign Ends"

Elated, Anna puttered in her garden, happy to run her hands through the soil once again. The old curse had been lifted.

~~~

In the next few months, Anna threw herself into the role of educating Lisa as though to mold her into the "right" kind of wife. She wanted to show her the things she knew so Lisa could take care of her boy, if Anna couldn't. Her breath caught. She closed her eyes and pictured her baby son, lying in his crib, so sweet, so innocent, so helpless. She had failed one child. Maybe she could make up for it somehow with Kevin and this new "daughter."

"I found a pattern for your wedding dress." Anna waved the packet at Lisa as she came into the girl's room, where she was sitting at the sewing machine. "Look, isn't this just elegant?" Pointing to the picture of a formal, high-necked, frilly and lacy dress, with leg-o-mutton sleeves, she smiled.

Lisa looked from the pattern to Anna, her eyes wide. "Wow, this is really gorgeous..." She paused and swallowed. "But it looks like it would be really hard to make—all those ruffles and lace..."

"No, no. We can do it." Anna swept clothing off a chair and sat down. "I saw the most beautiful satin in the fabric store in Billings. We should go look at it, soon."

"Well... actually, this is really a bit too fancy for me. I'm just a simple 'hippie chick,' you know." Lisa laughed. "I think I'd like to go look for a dress on my own, something less formal."

Anna's neck grew hot, the warmth radiating up into her cheeks. What? This girl didn't want Anna to make her wedding dress? The idea wouldn't penetrate her understanding. "But... I'm happy to make you this dress. I'd really like to..."

"Thank you, Mother Moser. I appreciate that, and I know you're a beautiful seamstress. But I really want to pick out my own dress. I hope you understand."

Anna rose from the chair, the pattern falling to the floor, the gray mist threatening to surround her once again. All she wanted was to be a mother and have someone to take care of. She blinked, seeing Lisa's eager, radiant face. *Oh no—I'm doing it again.*

She smiled at her future daughter-in-law, her heart contracting. The memory of the excitement for her own wedding flashed in her mind. She'd had to compromise and be married in a navy blue dress because shortage of dress goods after the war. This girl should have the wedding dress she wanted.

Bending down, she picked up the pattern. "You know, that's a very good idea. I want you to be happy with your dress, and with your life—here—with us."

Lisa reached out and enveloped her in a hug. "Thank you, Mother Moser. That means a lot to me."

"Please call me Anna." She squeezed back, new joy filling her heart. She took a breath and squared her shoulders. *I do not want to make the same mistakes with this new daughter-in-law as I did with my own daughters...* and Nettie had made with her.

~~~

"Gosh, your mom is such a worry-wart, so hung up on details." Lisa poured Monica a cup of coffee when she arrived for a visit.

"Oh, I know. Wedding plans—everything down to the nth degree?" Monica grinned and rolled her eyes with the image of Mom taking charge of sewing Monica's wedding dress.

"Yeah." Lisa scrunched her face into a scowl.

"She likes to have all her ducks in a row, that's for sure." She settled at Lisa's kitchen table with her coffee. "I used to hate it—really resent her constant meddling—but I've come to realize she needs to feel like she's in the driver's seat. And I think her compulsion goes back to her life in Germany during the war when she wasn't in control of very much."

Lisa nodded. "She's told me a few things about not having enough to eat and her mom selling off jewelry to buy food."

"I don't know all the details of her life there. She doesn't talk about it much. But I know she saw horrible things when she was a nurse—all the wounded soldiers and with no penicillin then…" Monica grimaced.

Lisa sipped her coffee. "It's really cool how she and your dad met though, when he was visiting a friend in the hospital."

"Yes, I think of it as a sweet romance and an answer to prayer for a better life. But then it took her two years to wade through all the paperwork and red tape before she could even come here."

"That must have been excruciating. I can't imagine being away from Kevin for that long."

"Me too, to be separated from Tom. No way." The wall clock ticked off several long seconds. Monica sighed. "And that was just another example of someone else having command over her life. No matter how she filled out the papers, there was always one more copy needed or a whole new sheaf of regulations that she had to fill out by hand, of course—no copy machines back then. And she had to travel about thirty miles by train to Frankfurt every time. She was terribly frustrated."

Lisa gave a low whistle and shook her head.

"But then, think about when she gets here." Monica grabbed a chocolate chip cookie, took a bite, and chewed slowly. "It's November, cold and snowy—she knows no one except this man she hasn't even seen for two years, and she goes out to Ingomar, Montana—even more 'middle of nowhere' than Horse Creek— to live with her in-laws. With no electricity and an outhouse! She doesn't speak much English, the culture and customs are so different, and everybody still thinks of the Germans as 'the enemy.' I think I would've been considering packing up and going back. But she didn't. She stuck it out."

"Must have been true love. And a big dose of courage." Lisa smiled. "Yeah, she did a really hard thing. I don't think I could've done it."

"Me either."

"That explains a lot." Lisa took a breath. "I need to try to be more patient with her."

Monica gazed out the window at the vast prairie horizon. "I wonder, why do we woman always struggle for control?"

CHAPTER EIGHTEEN

Lisa and Monica bent their heads over a wedding booklet's rules for a successful wedding. Anna was silent as the two laughed over the proper sequence of events. Then she chuckled too, happy that Monica had come to visit for a few days while Tom was gone on a business trip. Soon she was caught up in wedding plans, too, laughing joyfully, forgetting her pain and grief of the past.

"Nine months ahead—order the dress, six months ahead—order the invitations, then three months ahead—make appointment with the manicurist ... " Lisa giggled. "With my friends, it would be like 'Let's get together at Luke's Tavern tomorrow afternoon for a wedding.' September is only a month away. I guess I'd better get the invitations picked out!"

"Oh!" Monica waved her oatmeal cookie. "I was in this little boutique the other day and saw the perfect Gunne Sax wedding dress. It's you, it really is."

"Yeah? Maybe we could go to Billings this week, and we'll get all that done."

Anna's stomach knotted. So much for *her* ideas. Get two girls together and they're kindred spirits. Monica says one thing, and Lisa is off to town. *Let me suggest something and it's only an old lady's old-fashioned ideas...* She got up from the table and started clearing the coffee cups away. Then she paused at the sink. *Now wait just a second, Frau Moser. You told yourself you weren't going to do this anymore. Keep this up and you'll drive them both away.* She took a breath, surprised to find that she already missed them with the thought of them going away for a day.

Lisa got up from the table and came to stand beside her. "Hey, why don't the three of us go to Billings."

162

"Yeah, Mom." Monica stood too. "A girls' shopping trip."

Anna nearly dropped a cup. *Me? They're inviting me along?* "Well... ah...Yes, great. That sounds like fun." Her heart fluttered, and her legs wanted to dance.

~ ~ ~

Anna rode with the two young women to Billings the next day, the three discussing wedding plans and laughing over the silliest things. She hadn't had so much fun in ages.

"What if we invited some of the German relatives to come?" The idea just popped into her mind.

Lisa glanced at her in the rearview mirror. "Sure, that'd be great."

"Do you think anyone would come?" Monica turned toward Anna in the back seat.

She shrugged. "Probably not. But it might be nice to ask."

At the newspaper print shop, they ordered simple but elegant invitations, which would be sent to the ranch in a week. Then they stopped at the lunch counter at Newberry's Department Store for a bite to eat.

"We could look at dresses here," Anna suggested.

The girls exchanged a look, but Lisa nodded. "Sure, as long as we're here, let's do it."

Anna saw several gowns she thought were simply beautiful, but Lisa shook her head. "Too formal."

"They're not you," Monica agreed. "Let's walk down the street. There might be a Gunne Sax boutique here, too."

And there was. The girls both homed in on a simple white gown with a teardrop neckline, lace sleeves and overskirt. Lisa tried it on. When she came out of the dressing room, Monica gasped. "That's it! It's gorgeous."

Lisa twirled in front of the mirror. "It fits just perfect."

Anna started to say, "Isn't the neckline a little low?" but caught herself before she uttered the first word.

"What do you think, Mother Moser... Anna?"

Anna smiled at the beaming young woman. "I think you're beautiful in this dress."

~~~

The September day dawned warm and sunny for the outdoor wedding at Lisa's parents' house in Sand Coulee. Lisa's sister was maid of honor and Monica a bridesmaid. Tom stood up as best man for Kevin, and Lisa's brother was an attendant.

Anna's heart felt full once again as she watched her daughter and son-in-law walk forward to join Kevin and the minister under a ribbon and flower-bedecked archway. She drew in a sharp breath as Lisa came up the aisle on her father's arm. Her new daughter. So lovely. She squeezed Neil's hand. What a great family they had.

After the simple ceremony, everyone gathered for a roast pig barbecue and then danced to music by a group playing guitars, fiddles, and accordions.

"You should take your fiddle out and play again," she told Neil as they twirled around the garage dance floor.

He chuckled. "Oh, it's been so long since I've played—I've probably forgotten how."

~~~

The German relatives weren't able to make the trip on such short notice. Anna had worried what they would think about Kevin's long hair if she sent pictures of the wedding. But she bit her tongue and mailed them off anyway. She was just happy to have Kevin back home and a new daughter-in-law to teach about ranch life.

The months flew by, with a visit from Monica and Tom at Christmas, and then the wonderful news in spring—Lisa was pregnant. Anna couldn't help smiling. A grandchild. How perfect. Life was good again.

CHAPTER NINETEEN

Anna lowered the blue tissue-thin letter from her sister, Elsa. Her heart beat fast as she gazed at Neil across the dinner table.

"What's wrong, honey?"

"They're coming! Elsa and Albert are coming *here*. In September." Her mouth quivered upward into a half-smile, which she quickly covered with her hand. "*Ach, du lieber*, I can't believe it! They're coming *here*. To visit *me*." She shook her head in disbelief, then suddenly swung around, her gaze sweeping the house. "Oh my gosh, it's already June. I've got to get busy. The carpet... it needs cleaning... I have to strip the wax from this linoleum... we need to patch those tiles by the sink." She stood up, gathering the half-empty plates as though her sister were already on the way down the road from the store. "That mattress in Monica's old room... we should get a new one, and oh, the house needs painting outside."

~~~

Neil sat back, amusement etching his face as he watched his wife bustling from the table to the sink, running soapy water, muttering to herself, punctuating her activity with an ongoing list of things they needed to accomplish before their company from Germany arrived. It was as animated as he had seen her in several years. Ah, good. His letter to her sister, suggesting they come for a visit, had worked out just fine.

~~~

The mouth-watering aroma of sauerbraten lingered in the kitchen as Monica watched her mother and her aunt, heads bent close together, whispering in German, and then bursting into laughter. Her mom lifted a wineglass in salute, giving a toast that

165

Monica couldn't quite understand with her smattering of the language. But the laughter that followed was so contagious she couldn't help but join in. She glanced at her husband, sitting beside her. Tom was laughing uproariously, too, although he understood not a single word. He lifted his beer stein toward Albert's.

"Goot Beeer!" He tried to mimic the sound of the German words that were so close to English.

Albert's round, red face beamed. He chuckled, a deep, rollicking sound that came from his ample belly, then burst into song. *"Bier hier, Bier hier, oder ich fall um!"*

Monica caught Kevin's eye, and they both grinned. They had heard that little ditty often enough to know that, loosely translated, it meant "(More) beer here, beer here, or else I'll fall down." She interpreted for Tom, and for Lisa who sat looking a little bewildered, huge in her eighth month of pregnancy.

The background music stopped, and Anna jumped up to replace the record with one of spirited German folk songs. Sashaying back into the kitchen, she grabbed the plastic rings that had held a six-pack and stuck it on her nose, dancing and twirling with great flourishes. Elsa picked up her husband's cigar, threw an arm around Anna, and they began kicking their legs high in unison, like the "Rockettes." The men applauded.

Caught up in the spirit of the fun and laughter, Monica leaped from her chair to join in, also adorning her face with a plastic ring holder and giggling. A camera flashed as Lisa snapped pictures.

When the music stopped, the three women collapsed into their chairs, still laughing. Monica looked at her mother's glowing face under her cap of still-dark curls. She had never seen Mom let down her hair like this. She had never acted this happy and carefree, the lines in her face smoothed by laughter. She was an entirely different person.

The room was filled with the warmth of love and acceptance and camaraderie. There was nothing hidden. They were bound together as a family, and whatever their past or future problems, tonight everything was all right.

~~~

Finally, one chilly November day, Anna pressed her nose against the nursery window, simply staring at the pink bundle in the bassinet in front of her. Samantha Danielle Moser. *What a beautiful little being.* She watched in wonder as her granddaughter opened her tiny fists and scrunched them up again. The little red face puckered into a mass of wrinkles, and the rosebud mouth opened in a wail. A nurse appeared to gather up the bundle and motioned in the direction of Lisa's room.

She took Neil's hand and squeezed it as they walked down the hall. "Isn't she precious?"

"I know. I can't stop watching her." Neil squeezed back. "Sure brings back memories of when our babies were born." He slipped an arm around Anna's waist. "My beautiful wife, a grandma."

"Pfft." She waved the thought away with a flick of her wrist. "But I guess it's about time we have a grandchild. After all, we're both sixty."

Lisa was propped up on pillows, nursing the baby by the time they got to her room. Kevin sat next to the bed, his hand stroking the little head. "Do you want to hold her when she's done eating, Mom?"

Anna smiled, tears in her eyes. "Oh, yes. I'd like that. I'd like that very much."

~~~

Anna relished the cozy winter months, watching Samantha smile and coo. Her huge brown eyes reached out to her and warmed her heart with healing love.

Winter melted into spring, and one morning Anna stood outside the house, looking at her winter-trampled flowerbeds. Bitter-sweet memories once again flooded her mind as the eighth anniversary of Lizzie's death loomed. Her thoughts drifted back to when she was a little girl in Germany and the smell of warm loam as Papa worked the earth around his beloved rose bushes. It was almost time to try her yearly luck with her own roses in this arid wasteland. Every year she planted new bushes. If the drought didn't kill them, the grasshoppers ate them. If they did survive a summer, the winter killed them. Once in a while a bush or two would defy the odds and last into the next season. This gave her enough hope to continue to replant them, year after year after year.

She remembered, too, the first bouquet of sweetpeas brought to her on Mother's Day. Only now, in her mind, Lizzie had replaced Monica in this little ritual. She thought of the first year she and Neil were married, how she had welcomed the spring and the new life that it brought. Now it also brought sad memories of a life lost.

Plucking a weed, she shook her head. No, she wouldn't dwell any longer on the misery of the past. Now, she had a beautiful baby granddaughter, a new daughter-in-law, and her son was back home. Thank the Lord for the blessings that arose out of tragedy, like the phoenix from the ashes. Even though she had made terrible mistakes with her first-born and her last-born, perhaps she could make amends with little Samantha. What a beautiful baby—she made life worth living again.

CHAPTER TWENTY

The days turned into weeks, the weeks blended into months, and the seasons all became one. Somehow the '70s had become the mid-'80s. "Where did the time go?" Anna asked Neil. "Has it really been thirty-eight years since I came to this country?"

He shook his head and grinned. "Can't be. You're just as beautiful as that day I saw you step off the plane."

"You smooth-talker, you." She smiled and gave him a kiss.

Even though she wouldn't have needed to, Anna immersed herself once again in the hard labor the ranch demanded, enjoying the fresh air and sunshine of being out in the fields with her husband and son. When she stayed in the house, she busied herself with cooking, baking, sewing and taking care of her precious Samantha as often as she could.

How the little girl reminded her of Monica at that age, first crawling, then toddling everywhere at top speed to explore everything. A big smile lit up her face whenever Lisa brought her over to visit "G'amma."

But as the summer wore on, she noticed a slowing, a weariness where energy had once bloomed. Was it that thing called "old age?" Anna grimaced. Sixty-two wasn't that old. But lately everything she did exhausted her. Her reservoir of energy seemed depleted.

She shut off the tractor, eased herself down, and slowly made her way toward the pickup, stopping as her breath caught in her chest. The cough racked her body, from the depths of her soul, harsh, dark, and painful. She bent forward, shaking from the spasms.

Neil came running. "Honey, are you all right?" His anxious gaze searched her face as he encircled her with one arm and helped her into the pickup. "That's a nasty cough. Let's get you home. I think you've been working too hard. It's time for a rest."

"Oh, I'm fine. Just a little short of breath. Must have caught a cold when we were in Foster the other day." Anna sat up a little taller. "We've got to get this haying done. I'll be okay."

But she allowed herself to be led to bed when they reached the house, not protesting as Neil pulled up the covers. "Take a little rest. I'll fix dinner. Then I need to drive over to the south fields and see how Kevin's doing. I'll have Lisa come over to check on you later."

~~~

Never had Anna felt so listless, so tired, so sick. She had always gotten up and worked, through coughs and colds, stomach flu or cramps. It wasn't in her nature to "take things easy." But now, she just couldn't. This darn flu was not going away.

Lisa hovered and watched with a worried frown for two weeks, then insisted, "I think we'd better take you to town to see the doctor."

Doc Farnum had retired, so they drove in to see the new doctor in Foster. He prescribed antibiotics, and Anna came home, determined to tough it out. But they didn't seem to help.

One morning she awoke with blood in her mouth. She rinsed it out. Her gums were dark blue and bleeding. Fear sparked through her chest. She looked down at the purple bruise on her arm. That seemed to be happening so often lately, too, almost to the touch. Trying to remember what she'd learned from nursing nearly forty years ago, she shook her head. None of her experiences spoke to this problem.

She dragged herself to the breakfast table. "Why don't I feel better?"

"I'm worried about you, hon. You've always gotten over colds and flu so quickly—usually don't even catch 'em." Neil smoothed his hand over her forehead. "And you've still got a fever. I'm going to call the doc again."

The young doctor listened to Neil's concerns. "Well, it's probably just a virulent bug. After all, she is sixty-two and probably isn't able to fight it off as well as she used to. But, the bleeding gums and bruising causes me some concern. I think you need to see a specialist in Billings. I'll get you a name."

~~~

Neil's heart constricted as he watched the doctor in Billings poke and prod at Anna and ask endless questions. The testing went on and on. The nurses in the lab drew blood. Over the next three days they waited, and she had to go back for additional tests. Then they waited some more. Anna shook with exhaustion. Neil watched her with a feeling of helplessness. Just the three-hour drive from the ranch this morning seemed tiring enough for her. Now all this. Between tests, she leaned back in the stiff, hard chair in the waiting room, dozing off.

Neil thumbed through magazines, chewing his lower lip as he watched his wife, so gray, so gaunt. He hadn't noticed until now how much weight she'd lost. *What is this thing that has such a stranglehold on my wife? I shouldn't have let her work so hard.*

The doctor stepped out of his office. "It'll take a while to get the results of the tests. Can you come back in tomorrow?"

"What do you think it is, doctor? Do you have any idea?" His eyes bore into the physician's.

"It's too soon for me to make any diagnosis. I'll have to wait to see the results of the tests. Go ahead and make an appointment with the receptionist for tomorrow afternoon." He turned abruptly and walked away.

What the...? How rude. Neil clenched his fists and took in a deep breath. Anna was in no shape for the drive home and then back again the next day. He rented a motel room nearby. She fell asleep immediately as he held her tightly in his arms.

~~~

"Your blood tests show a low hemoglobin count and your white blood count is very high. I'm concerned that your viral infection has gone on so long. We've ruled out mononucleosis, aplastic anemia and lupus with the blood test…" He paused for a moment and flipped through the papers on his desk. "What I'd like to do next is have a bone marrow biopsy done. Let me call my associate in the oncology department and see when we might schedule one."

Anna stumbled into the waiting room and sat down heavily. Her mouth was dry, her gums painful. She swallowed hard. "Did he say oncology?"

Neil nodded, his lips tight, face gray under his field tan.

"That means… ca-cancer, doesn't it?" Her hands began to shake as they rose toward her face. She covered her mouth, her eyes filling with tears.

"Now, now. He didn't *say* that. I think they just want to do more tests, rule out… things." He swallowed, his Adam's apple bobbing, and took her hand in his, caressing it gently. "Don't worry, honey. It'll be all right. The doctors know what they're doing."

But Anna's mind reeled. *No. It's not all right.* Cancer. The word everybody feared the most. She thought of all the articles she'd read in *Prevention Magazine*, the vitamins she'd started taking to keep her healthy. Great clawing tendrils of fear raked through her intestines. She clung to Neil's hand, swallowing the sobs that threatened to break through.

"Let's not call the kids till we know for sure," she said.

Two days later, she lay in a hospital bed, staring at the stark white walls, fear growing larger like wildfire inside. She'd been admitted for an overnight stay, and the oncologist had drilled a tiny hole into her breastbone to extract bone marrow. Her chest was sore, and now she was waiting, yet again. *Why? Don't these doctors know what they're doing?* These past few days had been excruciating. No one was telling her anything. Just poking her with more needles and telling her to be patient. Hurry up and wait. Waiting was more painful than the drilling into her chest.

Neil stepped back into Anna's room, holding a white plastic cup of coffee. The oncologist followed him in and sat down next to her bed, thumbing through the chart.

~~~

Four hundred miles to the west, Monica gripped the receiver with a white-knuckled hand. "What...? Leukemia?" She sat down, suddenly feeling very weak. Tom poked his head around the corner of the kitchen, wide-eyed at her outburst. After a few minutes, she lowered the phone into the cradle.

Her hands trembled. "Mom's in the hospital in Billings, and they're going to start chemotherapy right away. They have to kill off all her blood cells in order to get the cancerous ones. Oh my gracious."

She crumpled in the chair, tears streaming down her cheeks. Tom knelt by her side, taking her in his arms.

~~~

Anna wasn't able to sleep. She turned her head toward the window. It was still dark outside, and the nurses wouldn't be in for a while yet. She swallowed. Her mouth was cottony. Her face felt shrunken, skin stretched taut over the bones. Her eyes scanned the room for the thousandth time. She lingered on the webbed crack in the wall next to her head. It was still there ... not going anywhere.

After a while, her gaze moved to the blue pump beside her bed, infusing her blood with chemicals so toxic that her immune system was now totally compromised. Before being allowed into the room, nurses, visitors, even Neil, had to mask, cap and gown like a surgeon, then scrub their hands with special antibacterial soap. Her eyes glanced with distaste at the bedside tray where they placed the food she could not eat, then skipped to the chart on the wall where they posted each day's blood test results, as the chemotherapy ate away at her.

How had this happened? She'd been so healthy all her life—never smoked, drank very little, always ate good healthy foods they'd raised themselves. She'd gone from what Neil jokingly called "pleasantly plump" to this weak, wraith-like bag of bones. Only a few thin, gray strands remained of her once thick, dark, curly hair. Her energy, her spirit, her spunk—all gone. A tear leaked from the corner of her eye and dissolved into the pillow.

She wracked her brain for the accomplishments in her life, anything she'd done to make a difference anywhere, to anyone. She swallowed past a painful lump in her throat. Would anyone miss her when she was gone? She'd only succeeded in alienating all her children at one time or another—maybe she was being punished for that.

The once-intermittent rumble of fear inside her was now a constant roar—this great beast had teamed up with the chemicals, trying to kill her. Clutching the sheets with clawlike fingers, she cried, "*Ach, mein Gott,* I'm not ready to die."

~ ~ ~

Monica's heart galloped in her chest. She felt both dread and excitement as she washed her hands outside the door of her mother's room. She took a mask from the box, and tied it with shaking fingers. With deliberate slowness, she turned the knob, opening the door, afraid of what was on the other side. Her breath stopped momentarily when she saw the pale, thin woman lying in the bed, hooked up to tubes, machines blipping and beeping beside her. She stretched her lips into a frozen smile to keep them from trembling. Then she stepped softly to the side of the bed.

Her mother's eyes opened at the rustling sound, uncomprehending for a moment, before she recognized Monica. "Oh, my dear. I'm so glad you came." Her voice was like a rusty gate hinge. She reached out a hand.

Monica took it in both of hers. Oh, poor Mom. She looked like… like death. No, it couldn't be… But she breathed deeply and forced herself to smile. "Well, this is one heck of a way for you to get a vacation."

Her mother grimaced, as though in pain. "I guess so." She gazed up at her daughter. "How are you doing, honey? How was your trip?"

"Oh, just fine. We got in about midnight last night and had to set up our booth at the trade show, so we didn't get to sleep till about two. And we hadn't had supper yet, so we stopped at the convenience store and bought one of those cardboard pizzas. Actually, I think the box would've tasted better." She forced a cheerful tone and chattered as though her insides weren't churning like the cream her mom used to make into butter. Maybe if she didn't talk about this … this thing, it would go away.

"It was such a great coincidence this show was scheduled in Billings. We'll be here over the weekend, so I'll be able to slip away and come visit you for a while every day."

"I'd like that. I'm glad your new business is going well." Her mother closed her eyes in weariness and dozed for a few minutes.

Before she left the hospital, Monica stopped by the cafeteria to find her dad, who was pushing a hunk of meatloaf around on his plate. Startled at the amount of gray in his hair, the haggard look on his weathered face, she stopped for a moment to steel herself once again.

He smiled when he saw her, stood, and wrapped his arms around her in a long hug, as if he needed to refuel his own strength from her. "It's good that you're here." He swallowed hard. "I'm so worried about your mother. I need to go to the ranch, help Kevin with some chores. Can you spend the day with her tomorrow?"

She nodded. "What are the doctors saying? Is this chemotherapy going to work?"

"I sure hope so." Her dad rubbed his callused hands over his face. "They hope it will kill all the leukemia cells, and if she doesn't get an infection—" his voice broke, "then it's possible she'll go into remission and begin to build up her system on her own again."

Monica squeezed his forearm. "It'll work, Dad. I know it will." She forced a cheery smile. "Well, I gotta get going. I'll come back in the morning. Have a good trip to the ranch. Drive carefully. Tell Kevin hi."

She stumbled out of the hospital, fear knotting her stomach.

The next day, on the way to the hospital, she stopped and bought some magazines and a newspaper to read to her mother. Together, they watched TV for a while, but her mom dozed often. Monica became restless and couldn't concentrate on the programs anymore.

A nurse came in to scrub down the room with disinfectant. Another brought in a silk plant a neighbor had sent. "Can't allow real flowers in here," she explained. She took Mom's blood pressure and temperature, then bathed her face with cool water. "Your temperature is up a little." She turned to Monica. "I'll leave a cool wet washcloth for her, and you can rinse it out now and again."

Monica draped the cloth over her mother's forehead and gently caressed her bare head. Her mom's eyes opened. "Thank you dear. I'm feeling better now. I'd like to sit up a while."

Monica helped her into the easy chair by the bed and read an article aloud from *Good Housekeeping*. She looked up to make a comment on what she'd read and saw tears flowing from her mother's eyes.

"What's the matter, Mom?" She moved closer and put a comforting hand on her arm.

"Oh, nothing, dear." Her mom shook her head. "This is all a little overwhelming." A weak smile touched her lips. "Don't worry about me. This treatment is working. I can feel it."

Monica stroked her mother's arm gently. She was afraid to get too close, afraid she might spread germs from her clothes. What could she say? Fear blocked her words. It sure didn't look like everything was going to be okay. Again, the voice inside her told her that if she didn't talk about it, it wouldn't be true. She took a deep breath.

"Yes, you'll be just fine, Mom. I know it. You'll be up and dancin' a jig again in no time! Just like when *Tante* Elsa was here." She tried to laugh, but she stopped abruptly, afraid that the chuckle would emerge as a sob.

In a little while her mother straightened. "I'm tired now. I'd better lie down again. Will you help me back into bed?"

Monica withdrew her arm, her sleeve now damp with her mother's tears. She steadied her as her mom shuffled to the edge of the bed. Lifting Mom's legs up onto the mattress, she tucked the sheet around her.

Monica's chest tightened as she looked at her mother lying there. She was so thin. She didn't look like Mom anymore. Her mind reeled. Nausea rose into her throat. Not enough air in the room. She couldn't stay there a minute longer. She looked out the window at the navy shadows that dusk cast over the snow.

"Well, Dad should be back pretty soon. I need to go back and get ready for the trade show banquet." She rubbed her hand over her mother's foot. "I'll be back tomorrow."

Tossing her mask into the wastebasket outside the room, she ran from the hospital, barely containing her sobs until she reached her car.

~~~

Anna stared out at the grayness of the descending night. She listened to the whooshing beat of the pump, picturing the toxic liquid dripping into her veins, scouring them empty. It could help her, or it could kill her. She was at the mercy of this beast, eating away inside her. She was so tired, but she knew she wouldn't sleep....

CHAPTER TWENTY-ONE

Anna tried to think of the positive—that this treatment would put her into remission and she would be able to go back to her normal life with Neil. Being able to work alongside her husband, even in the winter, when it was so cold and such a struggle to get out to the pasture to feed the cows. Getting up at dawn to bale the hay while it still had a bit of dew on it so all the dry leaves wouldn't be lost. Working out in the sunshine, driving tractor, hoeing her garden—she loved that part of her life.

She was not ready for her life to be over. In a couple of weeks, she would be sixty-three. That wasn't old, was it? There were too many things she hadn't done, too many things she hadn't said to her family. That quilt for Samantha wasn't finished. There was a pile of mending to be done. And, she'd really like to have at least one more garden. Maybe the roses will have survived this winter.

Anna shivered—so cold. No blood left in her to keep her warm. It was all dead.

Then she dreamed she was lost in the desert, the sun burning the bad cells out of her body. She awoke for a moment to feel the nurse bathing her face with cool cloths before she slipped away again, floating on a cool river, the lush green banks slipping by, people dressed in white gauzy dresses, waving at her from the shore.

~~~

"I'm afraid she's picked up an infection." The doctor wouldn't look Neil in the eye, but stared at his charts as if looking for the answer there. "It's a common occurrence in this treatment, of course, because the chemicals affect the immune system."

Such heaviness washed over him. All at once he couldn't hold himself upright. He had to sit down. He reached for a chair. "What can you …? Can you do … anything?"

"We'll be giving her a strong course of antibiotics, and we'll need to seal off her room. Only capped, gowned and gloved individuals allowed in. You can be there, if you'll comply with the sterile environment."

Neil nodded. "Of course. My… Our kids… I think I should call… "

"She's in a coma now. It might be a good idea to prepare them." The doctor reached out a tentative hand to give Neil a perfunctory pat on the shoulder, then turned and walked away.

He hunched in the chair, unable to stand. *Oh, dear God, please don't let her die.* Tears trickled down his face and speckled his jeans.

~~~

Monica entered her mother's room, rustling in the sterile paper gown, a surgical cap covering her hair, a mask over her nose and mouth, latex gloves on her hands, and paper booties over her shoes. Her chest was tight. She was suffocating. Her dad gave her a hug, his eyes blinking behind his glasses.

She walked to the bed, where tubes and machines connected her mother to life, and took a bony hand in her latex-covered ones. "Hi, Mom. I'm here with you now. I love you. Please don't leave us."

Her mother's breath came in tortured gasps.

Monica turned to her dad, tears streaming now. "Oh my God, I've killed her," she cried. "I was with her all that day when I was coming down with a cold, and I didn't know it. I just knew it wasn't sterile enough in here!"

Her dad enveloped her with his muscular arms and together they sat, listening to the whump of the pump and the beep of the monitors, drawing comfort from each other. Trying not to think of the inevitable.

~~~

The next day, Kevin arrived, feeling like a ghost in his sterile garb. His eyes searched his sister's and dad's. He reached for their hands and gave them a quick squeeze, then stepped to the bed. This was the first time he'd seen his mother since she'd gotten sick. The sight of her gaunt face, the slack jaw, the wizened arms and hands delivered a knockout blow to his solar plexus. He felt the color drain from his face, the energy from his body. His legs wouldn't hold him any longer. He slumped over the arm of the recliner next to the bed. Thoughts raced through him. She was going to die. He had caused this with his drinking and running away and not loving her like he should have. *Is she really going to die?*

Through his pain, Kevin became aware of Monica gently rubbing his back, his dad squeezing his arm. He reached out for his mother's hand. "Oh, Mom. I'm so sorry I left you," he whispered, "but I'm back now—to stay." For just a moment, he thought he felt pressure in return. "If you can hear me, I'm going to pray."

The three joined hands around the bed, and bowed their heads.

~~~

The river had changed. Now Anna was floating on a soft, white cloud, the figures in white holding hands in a ring around her. A soft, amber light suffused the cloud. She felt at peace, no longer sick, no longer bitter, no longer depressed. She smiled. "I'm going to be with Jesus at last. And with Lizzie—I'll get to see Lizzie again. Yes, I am … I'm ready."

As she floated with an angelic apparition beside her, the clouds parted slightly, and she gazed down, into a hospital room. A bald woman lay there, her skin hanging slack on her bones, tubes sticking out of her arms. A jolt of recognition passed through her. That was her. She stared at the vision. Who was that in the room with her? She couldn't recognize them; they were all shrouded in white gowns. Were they angels? Was she already dead?

"Our Father, who art in heaven... "

There! That was Kevin's voice.

"Oh, my sweet baby boy. He's come to see me. Oh, I've loved him so. He just doesn't know it." Once again she saw him as a little boy with the guitar he'd made from a hubcap and a two-by-four.

"Thy will be done..."

Yes, there was Neil, of course. "My loving, loyal husband. Always there for me." The vision of his broken spectacles when she first met him in Germany made her smile. She would miss him.

"Forgive us our trespasses..."

And next to them was Monica. "My beautiful daughter, so good, so accomplished. Does she know how proud I am of her?" Anna's heart softened, remembering her joy from Monica's music, her stories.

"For thine is the kingdom and the power..."

"No! None of them know. I've never told them how much I love them, how proud I am of my family. I can't leave them now. I can't go with you just yet. I have to tell them, just one time before I go. Oh, will they ever forgive me?"

Anna's eyes fluttered. Her parched lips opened. "...forgive me?" she whispered in a raspy murmur. The apparitions in white surrounding her bed leaned closer.

"Forgive us..." "We love you, Mom." "I love you, my darling." The voices spoke in soft unison. Hands squeezed hers and caressed her brow. She gave a sigh and drifted back into sleep.

~~~

Neil punched the nurse's call button.

"She came out of the coma for just a second and spoke," Monica blurted when the nurse entered. "Is that a good sign?"

The nurse smiled. "Yes, I would think so. Let me check her vitals. She does seem to be breathing a little better. Maybe simply having her family around her made a difference. Doctor will be in for his rounds a little later. We'll just keep an eye on her for now."

~~~

Neil's heart pounded as he entered the doctor's office, Monica and Kevin close behind. The doctor glanced up from his pile of charts and smiled, rising to shake each extended hand. "Well, well. Good morning, and it *is* a good one, isn't it?" He opened Anna's chart and studied it for a moment. "The good news is she's out of her coma and resting comfortably. I think we may have the infection under control—I want to give it a few days to make sure."

Neil nodded and looked at him expectantly, barely able to breathe.

"The bad news is that her white cell count is still too high."

Monica's eyes widened; she and Kevin exchanged glances.

"So…" The doctor thumbed through his chart again. "What I'm proposing is that we find a bone marrow donor. They've been having pretty good luck with that at some of the big hospitals."

"What does that mean?" Neil jumped in. "I'll be glad to donate marrow, blood, whatever…"

"Well, it's not quite so simple. We have to find someone who is immunologically matched. If she had a twin, that would be ideal. Usually a sibling comes the closest. Or if we could've gotten her into remission, we could've taken some of her own marrow. You see, we have to give her another round of chemotherapy, which kills off all the leukemia cells, and in the process, unfortunately, kills her own bone marrow. Then we must infuse the donor marrow into her bloodstream—kind of like planting a seed—and those cells go into the bone, where, in time, they will multiply and become functioning, cancer-free marrow."

"Her brothers and sister live in Germany." Neil's chest tightened.

"Hmmm. That does pose a problem. Well, the next best thing is children—are you two willing to be tested?"

"Yes!" Kevin and Monica answered at the same time.

~~~

"We have good news, Mrs. Moser," the doctor said, peering over his perpetually-held chart. "Your son has tested positive as a bone marrow match for you."

Anna opened her eyes wide and looked over the doctor's shoulder, where her gowned and masked family stood at the foot of her bed. She couldn't see their expressions, but searching Neil's eyes, she could see the smile crinkles at the corners. "Oh!" Her voice came out cracked and gravelly. "Good." Weakly, she lifted a hand. "Kevin, come…"

Her son, tall, slender, and she knew, handsome behind that mask, stepped closer to the bed, clasping her shrunken hand in his large, latex-covered paw. "Mom…"

"Do… you want… do this…? It's painful…" she rasped.

Kevin's hand tightened around hers. "Yes, Mom, I do. Don't worry about me. The pain's nothing, compared to what you've already gone through. I'm just so… so glad I can do this."

A tear trickled from the brown pools of his eyes into the corner of his mask. Her strong, silent son. Oh, how she loved him.

"Thank… you…." The effort of speech was just too overwhelming. As her eyes involuntarily closed again, she whispered, "Love… you …"

~~~

Kevin's hands shook as he left the room and stripped off the confining gloves, gown and mask. He had to get away from here, from everybody, from the smell of death. Outside, the fresh, cold winter air hit his lungs with a shock. He welcomed it. Lengthening his strides, he headed down the sidewalk, looking for a park, for some trees, some open sky, away from the claustrophobic buildings of the hospital complex. He needed his wife and baby. He would call tonight, ask Lisa to come.

Did he dare hope that his mother's body would accept his gift of marrow? Or would it be rejected, the cancer cells returning? She had said she loved him. He knew that, and yet had doubted it. He couldn't remember that last time he'd said he loved her. Why had he always felt smothered by her love and the need to run away? But it could be different now.

"Oh dear God," he prayed. "Give me the strength... No, give *her* the strength..."

~~~

Anna lay deathly still in the unyielding hospital bed. The nurse tried to make her as comfortable as possible. She turned her regularly to prevent bedsores and pneumonia, and checked her temperature and IV tubes. There was nothing else to do but to lie there and wait, her body spent from the chemical battle waged inside her. When she wasn't asleep, her mind traveled over the hills and valleys of her life. If only she could go back and talk to Mutti and Papa and tell them how much she loved and missed them. If only she could do things over again, maybe she could have related differently to her children. Maybe Kevin wouldn't have become estranged for so long. Maybe Monica wouldn't have moved so far away. Maybe Lizzie wouldn't be dead. The needle-like pain of her hatred for the Morgans gave her a shot of adrenaline.

In retrospect, she could see the events of her life like waves that had rolled her forward, one after another, building momentum, rising higher and faster, until they dashed her against this last shore of disease and death. She hadn't realized that by walling off her heart, she had doomed herself to a life only half lived, numbed with regret. She had tried to feel nothing, hoping that the absence of joy would be a fair trade for the absence of pain. But no, she *had* felt pain, and now she realized that being half alive was also being half dead. And, while giving in to death had been foremost in her mind for so many years, she now realized this was not what she wanted.

Grief still weighed upon her for the losses in her life—her fiancé Fritz, the soldiers who had died under her care during the war. The family, friends, and home she had left behind in Germany, her mother and father and her daughter, all dead. But this brush with her own death shocked her into dealing with the present rather than dwelling on the past. What could she do now, to make up for that past? "If only" was to look backward. She had an obligation now to look forward, to the future—if she ever got out of this hospital.

Love. That's what she felt now. An overwhelming, all-consuming love, as an antidote against pain, against all the tragic imperfections of life. There was only so much room in her heart. She could fill it with resentment or with love. And every resentment she allowed to remain took space away from the love.

Forgiveness. That's what her faith had taught her. She would be forgiven her failures. But how could she forgive the monster who had killed her daughter and nearly driven her insane? Was this possible?

~~~

Kevin watched his mother sleeping. She wasn't awake and lucid very frequently, but he was there as often as allowed.

The bone marrow harvest had been painful, all right. "This is going to hurt," the doctor warned. Kevin had grabbed the sides of the table, willing the pain out through his clenched fingers. The doctor pushed the hollow-cored needle, its sharp cutting edge boring through his skin, deep into his pelvic bone. Then again into his chest. "I'll need to take samples from several places to make sure I get enough," the doctor explained.

The very memory of it made him nauseous. But the pain and the twenty-four-hour stay in the hospital was worth every second if it could heal his mother.

He visualized the marrow cells entering Mom's bloodstream, traveling like a fleet of whitewater rafts down a river, each one splitting off into different tributaries, making their way into her bones. Then like the early settlers of America, they would set up camp, "homesteading" as it were, trying to establish fertile fields and families to produce new marrow cells.

Would they run into resistance, like the settlers, by attacks from his mom's own body, or would his donated cells be strong enough to overpower her natural defenses?

He shook his head to bring himself back to present. He'd almost drifted off to sleep, thinking. He had been doing a lot of that lately. And asking himself questions. Could this cancer be *his* fault? Why had he felt so smothered while growing up? Without knowing why, he'd built a dam around his heart, cementing it with the fear that even the slightest crack would sweep him away into a sort of madness his feelings created.

The wall had crumbled now, and grief and pain flooded him as he never allowed before. But instead of being unbearable, he was now sharply aware that she loved him, and he loved her, too. He was surprised to find he felt even more closeness and appreciation for his loving wife, Lisa, and for their precious two-year-old daughter, Samantha.

Mom had been so terribly unhappy for so long. People had never accepted her for who she was—she had always been "that German woman," different, alien, on a different plane. And so, her kids were branded in the same way. Kevin's heart was pierced with pain as he remembered the hazing he'd received in school. No, her illness wasn't his fault.

He stood up from the easy chair and stretched his long legs, ambling slowly to the window to watch the snow melting on the sunny side of the building. "I am who I am. And she is who she is," he said out loud to the blue sky. And there was nothing wrong with that. Could they accept that in each other?

~~~

Neil took over the watch as Kevin left to get something to eat. The days stretched into eternity for him, watching his beloved Anna lying so still, the chemicals pumping into her body, the machines keeping her alive. He talked to God constantly, beseeching Him to give her another chance, hell, to give *him* another chance. All his perceived failures—his lack of direction, his inability to protect her from hurt, his lack, somehow, to fix any of this—marched past him in slow motion. If she got well, could they both accept that failure was bearable, and simply start over?

There was more to life than working all the time. They would take more time together. They would travel more. They could go back to Germany. Dance. Sing. Talk more. Yes, that was his shortcoming, but he would see to it that they would talk more.

He caressed her hand, and she opened her eyes for a moment and smiled.

~~~

It was Monica's turn to sit by her mother's bed. She tried to read a book, then tossed it aside, and picked up a magazine. Flipping through the pages without seeing them, she jumped up from the chair and paced to the window, then to the door, and back to the bed. These past few weeks away from her husband and her home were beginning to wear. Waiting. More waiting. It was like being suspended just above a fire, not knowing whether it was going to catch hold and grow, it's hot fingers grasping her, or if it would die down, gradually subsiding into a warm, comforting glow.

"Is this transplant going to work?" she asked the nurse who came in to check on her mother. "How long will it take before we know?"

The nurse shrugged. "It varies. It could be a couple of weeks or it could be a month. Doctor will be taking another bone marrow sample in a few days."

Fear iced Monica's blood. She couldn't sleep. She had no appetite. What more could she do? It was just another one of her failures that her bone marrow hadn't been a match. After all, she was the one who probably had caused the infection that had almost killed her mother. She had to do something to make it up. She'd never been quite good enough, strong enough, worked hard enough, sacrificed enough. And if her mom died… Her head jerked. No. That thought was not allowed. It had just sneaked in. But it must not surface again.

~~~

Anna sat upright, propped with pillows, the head of her bed elevated. She was able to stay awake for longer periods now, and carry on parts of conversations at least. Today, Neil, Monica, and Kevin were allowed in to see her at the same time. At last, they were together as a family. She was at peace.

She knew God had forgiven her. For the first time in years, she could think of Lizzie without feeling rage against Jeremy and Hank Morgan—rage that had consumed her for so many years. Best of all, her family had forgiven her for being so controlling, so obsessed. She searched each face, the lines around Neil's eyes more relaxed, Monica's and Kevin's smiles soft with love.

The doctor stepped into the room, gowned, gloved and masked. She would recognize his eyes anywhere and wondered if she'd ever get to see his face.

He shook hands with everyone. "I'm here with good news." He looked down at his chart. "The latest test of your bone marrow shows no signs of leukemia cells. You are in remission."

Speechless, Anna again looked at her family's faces as the doctor spoke. Tears streamed from their eyes, and they came as one to hug her, to hold her. Then they were all laughing and crying at the same time. Anna kept thinking, *I'm going to live; I'm going to live! I've been given a second chance.*

CHAPTER TWENTY-TWO

The day Neil, Monica, and Kevin brought Anna home from the hospital, everyone laughed and talked and sang for the entire one hundred-fifty-mile trip—German folk songs, popular songs from the '60s and '70s, new tunes from the '80s that she didn't even recognize as music.

She simply nestled into the softness of the car seat, thoughtfully outfitted with extra pillows and a blanket, and watched the familiar landscape passing by as though it were a brand new vista. She had never seen it in this light before—the low, rolling hills like an old friend welcoming her, but at the same time the long, empty road stretched out ahead like the beginning of a whole new journey. All those years she'd wasted, thinking she hated this barren land, wishing for greener pastures, looking for the pot of gold at the end of the rainbow, when all the time it was right here within her grasp.

Neil pulled their white Mercury Cougar into the yard with a flourish, dust rising up behind. Kevin and Monica leaped out of the car, running to meet Lisa, Samantha, and Tom who had arrived ahead of them. Neil lifted Anna gently from the car and carried her to the house. She smiled up at him. "Just a year ago, you would've hurt your back trying this, or dropped me," she teased. He merely grinned back.

As they entered the house, Anna was momentarily blinded by the cool dimness so in contrast with the bright sun outside.

"Surprise!"

She gave a start. The living room was filled with people— Evelyn with arms outstretched, her husband Larry by her side; Gertie and Jack Sparks, both with big grins; the Edwardses clapping, even the whole Mitchell family—Emily radiant in a pretty red sweater. A huge banner spelling out "WELCOME" in sparkling letters hung from the wall. Anna took in balloons and flowers everywhere, and a table set with coffeepots, cookies, cakes and sandwiches. Neil set her down in the recliner. Her eyes spilled over with tears.

Evelyn ran up and knelt by the chair to give her a hug. "I'm *so* glad you're home. I was *so* scared." Her friend's eyes were red-rimmed, but she was smiling.

One by one, the neighbors shook her hand, gave her hugs and served her coffee, repeating the welcoming phrase, "We're so glad you're home."

Emily Mitchell was the last to leave. She paused at the doorway, took out an envelope, and handed it to Anna. "Thank you…" she hesitated, "for being a friend when I needed one. I'm happy you're okay."

After Mrs. Mitchell left, Anna opened the envelope with a curious frown and read:

Dear Mrs. Moser,

I want to apologize for being such a bully to Monica and Kevin when we were in grade school. I have so much respect for you and your family, and I am so very sorry that I caused pain to any of you. My best wishes for your health and recovery.

Sincerely,

Ben Mitchell

Her breath caught in her throat. This was the sweetest balm she could ever have received.

Afterwards, every time she thought of that welcoming gathering, tears filled her eyes again. They really *did* care about her after all. And the best part was that she now realized she cared about them, too.

~~~

The weeks went by, and with each passing day, Anna grew stronger. Each check-up through the summer and fall brought good news. Kevin's bone marrow had been a perfect match. The longer she went with no sign of recurrence, the better were the odds.

"But even if it does come back," she told Neil on the way home from a visit to the clinic, "I'm so thankful I've been given this second chance to look at my life differently and to get to know my kids again."

She'd had some long, intimate talks with her son, something she'd never been able to do before. Monica and Tom had been visiting about once a month, too. She felt closer than ever to her daughter. And, she had begun to appreciate both her son-in-law and daughter-in-law. They were warm and loving partners for her children and took good care of them. She didn't have to worry about that any more.

Neil reached for her hand and gave a squeeze. "I'm so very proud of you. You have been so brave and so strong." He swallowed. "I don't think I could've survived all this. I mean, what you went through, both physically and mentally."

A warm rush of love washed over Anna's heart. She knew it had taken a lot for him to say that.

~~~

She spent a lot of time the first several weeks sitting in the green and white webbed lawn chair on the porch, one of her crocheted afghans covering her lap. She drank in the warmth of the sun and the freshness of the air, reveling in being home again. Now and then she would pick up the garden trowel to turn the rich, black earth in a planter beside her.

The lawn was beginning to turn brown. Maybe she should start the sprinkler. Next summer, she'd be back out in her garden—she could hardly wait.

The horses kicked up their heels as they raced across the pasture, tails and manes streaming in the wind. The late spring day was warm and clear, the sky a vivid sapphire glow against the sun-drenched prairie grass.

She stretched her legs out in front of her and took stock of the years she'd lived here. All those years she had alternately fought the dirt and the withering heat and cursed the frozen wasteland, telling herself how much she hated it here. All the time she'd wasted feeling left out and unaccepted. Now she saw her life differently, as though she was looking through someone else's eyes.

Each little dusty nook and cranny of this house had her loving touch—the coats of paint, the endless hours of scrubbing, the little doilies she'd crocheted to give it that homey touch. Even the yard that would never stay green, the flowerbeds that curled and dried despite all the watering. She knew every mile of the fields she had driven the tractor over, pulling a plow or a rake or a baler, every coulee and hill of every pasture where a cow might be hiding with her newborn calf.

Anna recognized now that she loved this ranch as though it were one of her own children she had birthed. For she and Neil had, in a way, given birth to this ranch, nurtured, disciplined, fought for it.

As the days went by, she gradually began walking around the yard, stopping to study each tree she had planted, remembering the year she and Neil had dug the holes, inserting the spindly little twigs she dared not hope would survive. Not all of them had, but there were enough of them now to cast their twenty-foot shadows over the house during the hot days of summer.

The lilac bushes were large enough to shade the dining room window and she loved the smell of the blossoms in early spring. Tulip bulbs had pushed their way through the winter soil to peek out at the sun, and the hollyhocks—for so long the only flower she could count on—also beamed through pastel blooms at her.

She knelt beside a climbing rose bush and stroked the velvety red petals. Turning to gaze around the yard, she smiled at the bright proliferation of roses that had miraculously survived the winter.

Anna finally had her rose garden, just like Papa's.

Author Afterword

Although this book is based on my mother's life, I have used the creative liberty allowed by writing a fictionalized version. In real life, my mother died from her leukemia. With fiction, I was able to write the ending the way it should have been.

Many of the characters are fictionalized composites, including the character Lizzie.

If you enjoyed this book, please leave a review on Amazon or Goodreads or let me know through my website: www.heidimthomas.com

Coming Soon

Rescuing Samantha is part of the "American Dream" series, but begins the story of a new character, Samantha Moser, Anna's granddaughter. Samantha leases great-grandparents Nettie and Jake's ranch near Ingomar, Montana, with the dream of raising Thoroughbreds. The first brutally harsh winter brings changes in her life and her dreams.

ABOUT THE AUTHOR

Heidi M. Thomas grew up on a working ranch in eastern Montana, riding and gathering cattle for branding and shipping. Her parents taught her a love of books, and her grandmother rode bucking stock in rodeos. She followed her dream of writing, with a journalism degree from the University of Montana. Heidi is the author of the award-winning "Cowgirl Dreams" novel series and *Cowgirl Up: A History of Rodeo Women*.

Seeking the American Dream and *Finding True Home* are based on her mother who emigrated from Germany after WWII. She makes her home in North-Central Arizona.